Changed Somehow

THE POTTER'S HOUSE BOOKS TWO – BOOK 7

CHLOE S. FLANAGAN

NOTE FROM THE AUTHOR

The 24 books that form The Potter's House Books Series Two are linked by the theme of hope, redemption, and second chances. They are all stand-alone books and can be read in any order. Books will become progressively available from January 7, 2020.

Book 1: *The Hope We Share*, by Juliette Duncan

Book 2: *Beyond the Deep*, Kristen M. Fraser

Book 3: *Honor's Reward*, by Mary Manners

Book 4: *Hands of Grace*, by Brenda S Anderson

Book 5: *Always You*, by Jen Rodewald

Book 6: *Her Cowboy Forever*, by Dora Hiers

Book 7: *Changed Somehow*, by Chloe Flanagan

Books 8: *Sweet Scent of Forgiveness*, by Delia Latham

Books 9-24 to be advised

1

Floating on air is such a clichéd phrase.

But there really wasn't a more original way to describe the moment. In a few short months, she would finally see a theater poster with the words "Starring Natalie Rivers" printed on it.

Okay, so maybe after all this time, her face wasn't lighting up the "Great White Way" yet—yikes! another cliché—but the lead in the off-Broadway production she'd just landed was a compelling role. And that's what mattered.

In *The Seat Fillers,* her character, the neglected daughter of a Hollywood star, would overcome addiction and excess to help others in similar situations. Portraying the character before and after the transformation would require a lot of range. If she executed it right and captured the right people's attention, the part could make her career.

Descending from her cloud long enough to check the storefront signs around her, she realized she'd almost passed the dry cleaners. Once she spotted it, she hurried inside to pick up her boyfriend Sebastian's dry cleaning, rolling her eyes as she paid the steep price. There were at least a half dozen cheaper cleaners in the surrounding neighborhood, but he insisted on using what he thought was the best. She accepted the garments with a smirk. Oh well, it was his money.

The simple act of re-entering the warm, slightly humid midafternoon sunlight was enough to return her thoughts to the role. After the first audition, as with most of her auditions, she'd driven herself nuts trying to figure out whether the director had liked her or not. She'd done a scene from the beginning of the play when her character, Marissa, had just stolen money from her dad to buy drugs. In that moment, Marissa had been drowning in despair and self-loathing.

Then, the director had asked her to do a scene after the character got clean, a scene where she confronted the opportunistic drug dealer who supplied to underage kids in Beverly Hills. Marissa was now confident and fueled by righteous passion. The contrast was sharp, but Natalie had been almost certain she had nailed it.

Apparently, all those seasons of being a swing actor who embodied vastly different characters within the same production had paid off, because she got the callback.

She released a self-satisfied sigh and stepped off the curb across from Sebastian's apartment building, only to hear the screech of brakes followed by the blare of a horn.

"Watch where you're going, blondie!" the driver of the taxi that had nearly plowed into her leaned out his window and shouted. He finished the tirade with a few expletives and shook his fist at her.

Turning to face the cab head on, she looked the driver straight in the eyes and flashed the gradual, brilliant smile she'd practiced in front of the mirror for hours. She raised her head and slid her shoulders back, showcasing all her generous assets at once. Immediately, the driver stopped shouting, so she puckered her lips and kissed the air in his direction. His mouth fell open and his gaze, she didn't doubt for a second, followed her all the way across the street until she entered the building.

****

"I knew you'd get it!"

Natalie quirked her brow at Sebastian's enthusiasm. It wasn't like him to be encouraging. He was generally too self-absorbed for that. "Thanks, baby. I wasn't so sure."

He paced the room excitedly. "You were a shoo-in for a lead like that. I knew that when we first met." He stopped and faced her. "Marlowe is directing, right? Maybe you can talk to him about considering me for the play he's supposed to do next."

Ah. That explained his excitement. "Yeah, maybe in a few weeks, we'll be on those kind of terms."

His thin lips curled back over his perfect white teeth. "Now you're talking!"

Bounding across the room, he wrapped her in his arms and kissed her hard. The whole time, his hand snaked further and further down her back.

She was too good at her craft to squirm in his grasp, even though his attentions alternated between numbing and repulsive. Besides, what Sebastian didn't know was that—now that she wasn't in between parts anymore—she wouldn't need to stay at his place to save money.

Yeah, she'd be on the right terms with a well-known director soon, but she wouldn't stick around long enough for Sebastian to benefit from it.

2

One of the rookie actors actually applauded.

Natalie had just finished her first read-through of the pivotal scene in the play where Marissa hit the rocky bottom of her self-destructive lifestyle.

Staring up at the ceiling, arms outstretched and eyes damp, she cried, "I can't do this anymore!"

The scene ended, and the room was perfectly still—that is, until nineteen-year-old Ryan Fletcher started applauding from his place in the corner of the room.

Snickers ran through the other players and crew, but Natalie sent him an indulgent smile.

"All right, that's enough! Let's move on," Marlowe barked. "Fletcher!" He turned on the young man. "Since you have everyone's attention now, you can read next. Get over here."

Ryan's face reddened, but he hurried over and sat across the table from Natalie.

Her smile broadened. Normally, she wouldn't have much patience for some kid cast in his first major speaking part in a real play, but she'd always make an exception for an admirer.

Ryan settled into his chair and role. He slouched, making his already small frame seem even more waif-like. Then he began reading his lines in a cracking voice that made him sound more adolescent. Just like that, four or five years faded away and he was Liam, the misguided teenager.

"So what if it does kill me, Marissa? It's not like anyone will care!" he cued her, then stared straight at her, his deep blue eyes wide, pain-filled, and searching right through her.

A thick lump filled Natalie's throat and nearly choked off her breath. Still, his piercing eyes pulled on her. Why was he looking at her like that? So expectant and needy.

Her heart began to pound violently. *What was the line?* How could she forget? She always worked hard to know dialogue well enough to go almost entirely off book by the first rehearsal. Now she was scanning the script for the words as though she'd never seen it before.

Marlowe cleared his throat, which snapped her into focus enough to find her place.

"I—" It came out like a croak. She swallowed and tried again. "I care Liam. You matter to me, and I'll never let anything hurt you—even if that means protecting you from yourself."

It took all of her self-control not to wince at her own delivery. The words had mechanically slid out, like her tongue was a cheesy dialogue conveyor belt.

She glanced at Marlowe, who simply glared. Alec, the assistant director, cut in. "Why don't we press on? We need to block …"

"No!" Marlowe interrupted him. "No! Natalie, do that again. Ryan, cue her."

"It's not like anyone would care!"

She leaned forward, not bothering to look at her script. "I care! You matter to me, Tim—Liam! You matter to me, and I'll never let anything hurt you. Even if it means protecting you from yourself."

"Did I miss something here? Are we putting on a high school production?" Marlowe demanded. "Do it again!"

So she did again and again, each time sounding less believable than the last, until they finally moved on to another scene with different actors. She tried to pay attention, but panic churned in her stomach. What was wrong with her? Although Marlowe's high school drama remark stung, he'd been right.

A whole week of preparations, blocking scenes, and rehearsals went by, with Natalie polishing every part of her performance except the scenes with Ryan. For those, she could barely get through without stammering and getting panicky.

Finally, at the end of the fifth rehearsal, Marlowe pulled her aside in the hallway, leaving the door to the theater ajar such that the entire cast and crew could probably hear too. "Natalie, what is going on here? You are ruining the entire production with your performance in the Liam scenes."

"You could always cut that part out," she suggested.

"No, I'm not going to cut it out just because you have some kind of hang-up!"

"Then give me a little more time to work it out, please. I'll get there. I always do."

He crossed his arms and scowled. "No, I really don't think you will. I don't think you have the heart for this, Natalie."

"W—what do you mean?"

He threw up his hands. "Am I speaking Greek or something? I mean you're a faker, Natalie. You may call yourself an actor while you go around putting on a mask to pretend you're a queen or a doctor, or anything else, but you're really nothing but a faker. You don't have the heart or soul to actually *be* this part."

He pointed in the general direction of her midsection. "Something is missing there."

His words resounded through her, vibrating on her heat and pain receptors as if he had physically struck her, instead of merely insulting her.

Her hand went to her mouth. "That's not true. I—" She dropped her arm, whirled around, and ran for the exit.

"Where do you think you're going? Look, you cause me any more problems like this, and I'll see to it you never get cast in this city again!"

3

"I've got the blues," the lead singer of Natalie's favorite jazz band crooned through her earbuds.

"Isn't that the truth?" Natalie muttered as she threw diced ham, onions, and other vegetables into a cast-iron skillet and tossed them in oil.

She and Sebastian rarely ate in, so when the impulse to prepare a home-cooked meal had attacked, omelets were the only thing she could make with the hodgepodge of ingredients on hand in the kitchen.

After her confrontation with Marlowe, she had rushed home to the apartment, simultaneously exhausted and wound up. Now she was cooking for Sebastian—maybe for the first time in their four-month relationship—and listening to her music full blast in hopes of drowning out the director's words.

No heart.

She vigorously beat the eggs while the mixture in the skillet sizzled. Who was he to talk to her about heart? Everyone knew he was the type of director who delighted in bringing actors to tears with harsh critiques of their delivery. It was all in the name of excellence, people would say. He was one of the best because he expected 200 percent from his actors.

Maybe that was all that was behind his attack on her, too. Surely he wouldn't have pushed her like that if he hadn't thought he could prod her into a better performance.

She poured the eggs over the meat and vegetable mixture and

began tilting the pan to distribute everything evenly.

Maybe Marlowe thought he could make her excel. But could he? Her reaction to her scene with Ryan was terrifying. She had never experienced anything like it.

Well, that wasn't quite true. She *had* experienced something like it, but that had been a completely different situation. This wasn't some squiggly, needy infant she'd been dealing with; this was practically a grown man.

So what did it all mean? That she couldn't pull off a maternal role? At her age, that would wipe out about half of her potential roles within a couple of years.

The eggs were beginning to firm when a hand grabbed her shoulder. She jumped and spun around to face Sebastian.

His lips were moving, so she pulled out her earbuds. "What?"

He rolled his eyes. "I said, didn't you hear me come in?"

"No, and you startled me."

"Startled *you*? What about me? I thought I had stumbled into the wrong apartment. What are you doing at the stove?"

"Go wash your hands, idiot. It will be ready in a minute."

He didn't argue, and a few minutes later, they sat down.

"Hey, this is actually pretty good," he remarked.

"Thanks."

Good thing she wasn't feeling chatty, because he rambled about his day of auditions all through the rest of the meal and the dishwashing.

Afterwards, they sat down on the sofa.

He was still talking. "All I have tomorrow is one audition for a bit part in the new Denton production."

With a groan, he rested his elbows on his knees and began rubbing his forehead.

"What's the matter? Do you have a headache?"

"This whole business is a headache!"

She watched him dramatize over his lot in life for a while longer, then slowly reached her arms out to him. "Come here a minute."

He dropped his hands and looked confused. "Why?"

"Would you just come here?" She helped him relax into a reclining position with his head resting on her lap. Methodically, she began massaging his temples with even, counterclockwise rotations.

Circle. Circle. Circle. Gentle and concerned. *There.* Anyone from a mile away could see she was a warm and caring girlfriend.

The tiny muscles beneath her fingers tensed, and she refocused on his face. He was frowning up at her. "Hey, what's up with you tonight, Natalie? I didn't realize your Marissa character was some kind of June Cleaver role."

Immediately, her hands stilled. Geez, he was more perceptive than she gave him credit for. What was that old saying? You can't con a con?

"I don't have a role anymore," she admitted.

"What?" He sat up straight on the sofa and faced her.

She looked away and leaned back into the cushion, now 100 percent exhausted as she recounted her confrontation with Marlowe.

When she finished her story, he released a sigh. "Oh, I see. It's not like you lost the part or anything. I mean, Marlowe is being a total diva, but everyone knows he's like that. He can't just fire you, though."

Her lips went tight. "Maybe not, but I'm not going back to the play."

"Are you crazy? Nobody walks away from an Osborne Marlowe play. You'll never get work again!"

"I'm not sure I even care anymore."

"Do you hear yourself right now? What are you talking about?"

She stood up and faced him. "Would it kill you to give me a little support, and help me figure it out instead of rushing to judgment?"

"Figure what out?" He threw his hands up. "All I see is you getting hysterical because you had a little fight with the director. Deal with it! It happens all the time. You don't throw away your career over it. Working with him is going to open so many doors."

"Doors for you, you mean? Isn't that what you're thinking? You're waiting for me to get in good with Marlowe so I can talk him into giving you a chance!"

He sprang to his feet and stood toe to toe with her. "What's wrong with that? Isn't that what anybody would want? Let's face it, Natalie. You're a decent actress and a total hottie, but that's all you've got going for you. So if you get a chance like this, you really shouldn't mess it up. That would be stupid."

"A decent actress? What do you know about any of it? You

couldn't get a job handing out fliers without latching onto someone else's influence. You're just a spoiled rich kid living a pipe dream on his family's dime!"

His face went fiery red. "I never noticed you complaining about getting free room and board on that dime!"

She released a shuddering laugh. "Oh no, Sebastian, sharing a home and bed with you is a lot of things, but it's certainly not free."

At that, his complexion went from red to pale. "Then maybe you'd be happier finding someone better to sponge off!"

"Maybe! It wouldn't be hard! I'll leave tonight, in fact."

"Good luck! Just be sure and get your hands on his wallet before he figures out what a frigid jezebel you are!"

He stormed toward the door. "I'm leaving for an hour. When I get back, I expect you to be gone."

4

Of course it would be raining.

City rain always looked so romantic in the movies, but it wasn't. There was nothing romantic about water gushing from the sky like a busted pipe in a South Bronx apartment building.

It had only taken Natalie a half hour to pack her bags and leave Sebastian's apartment. Seething with rage had made her work incredibly efficiently, for some reason.

But now that she was outside, her mind was awash with the cold truth that she had no clue what to do next, apart from renting a bus station locker to keep her meager possessions safe until she figured it out.

The weather prevented her from taking the long walk she really needed, so she settled for taking refuge in a movie house that was showing an all-night independent film marathon.

Scores of men and women in business suits marched across the screen in the opening of the first film, an understated critique of corporate greed simply titled, *Heartless*. The plot and acting were not enough to hold her attention, though.

Heartless.

Marlowe had accused her of having no heart. Maybe he was right. Sometimes she wondered. And tonight, she wondered if she had a brain either. It had been stupid to pick a fight with Sebastian while she was without income. She had a little bit in the bank, but it wouldn't last long in Manhattan.

She'd probably have to get a motel room for the time being

since she didn't have any family or friends to stay with. Friends didn't come easily.

"I asked for that file half an hour ago!" the business executive on the screen bellowed at his assistant.

The assistant, played by a young blonde, wore a matronly cardigan with her hair swept up in a bun to make her look older, but her childish facial features belied the attempt.

Natalie studied the girl. She sort of resembled Kyla, the last person she had made friends with. Kyla was a cute, sweet eighteen-year-old actress just starting out. She and Natalie had worked together on a limited-run play several months before. As was often the case, Natalie had been between living arrangements when she met Kyla. Hearing that the girl was short a roommate in her Bronx apartment, Natalie had conveniently decided to get to know her better.

Kyla had been so grateful for Natalie's advice and occasional coaching that she had gladly agreed to let Natalie replace the missing roommate.

All in all, it had been a good symbiosis. Natalie had a cheap place to stay, and Kyla had benefited from her experience.

But then, Sebastian Claypool had walked onto the scene. He'd been cast in the play as a last-minute replacement. Kyla had been instantly enamored with the handsome actor with the toothpaste-commercial smile. What's more, he had really seemed to like her too, and they had dated for several weeks.

But right from the beginning, Natalie had noticed more than Sebastian's pearly whites. He always wore simple, yet high quality leather shoes and designer clothes. Then there was that old money Connecticut accent he could never completely conceal. All of those things had sailed over Kyla's head, but Natalie had recognized them for what they were: evidence that Sebastian had come from privilege.

It had been ridiculously easy to insinuate herself between the young couple and ensnare Sebastian. All it had taken was a suggestive look here, a little ego stroking there, with a provocative outfit or two thrown in for good measure, and Sebastian had dumped Kyla and asked Natalie to move in with him.

The young blonde actress on the screen fled to her desk and burst into tears to lament her plight as an underpaid, undervalued cog in the tyrannical wheel of her boss's money-grabbing enterprise.

Had Kyla cried after Sebastian left? She really was a sweet girl, who no more deserved Natalie's betrayal—yes, betrayal—than the poor girl on screen deserved her lot in life.

Was this what regret felt like? It seemed so strange. Ordinarily, she didn't spare time for such things. It had always been easy enough to justify her actions with a simple creed: The world is a nasty place and sometimes you have to be nasty to endure it. But this rationalization didn't feel as convincing as it once had.

To her relief, the young blonde actress's scene ended and Natalie let her mind become a blank as she finished the film and two others after that.

Hours later, when she left the theater, she had reached no definite conclusion except that she was ravenous, so she sloshed through puddles for several blocks until she reached an all-night diner.

5

The diner was empty, except for two female police officers, who sat at the counter and spared Natalie a glance before going back to their morning coffee.

She slid into a vinyl booth and studied the menu. It was usual diner fare.

In no mood to worry about her waistline, she ordered a hamburger along with a coffee to help take the edge off the chill the spring downpour had created. As she waited for her order, she took in the atmosphere. The air was heavy with the unmistakable smell of fried food and an undercurrent of something sweet and buttery. The delicious aroma was probably emanating from the display case of pies that stood in the corner.

It was just like Betty's.

The small town in upstate New York where Natalie grew up had offered few job opportunities for young people. But Natalie had found steady employment all through high school at Betty's Diner. She had even gone back to it from time to time when things got rocky in the city. Betty always welcomed her back, no questions asked.

The ashy, balding man that doubled as a waiter and short order cook set a large burger in front of her, but as she stared down at it, her appetite began to wane. With her finances in the state they were, there was a good chance she'd have to go back home now. Going back to wait tables at this stage of her career and life was embarrassing, yes, but the more disturbing part was the realization that she would have to go back to her mom's house too.

Wasn't her mom going to love that? After months without a phone call, Natalie would once again show up on the front doorstep asking for a rent-free bed.

She took a nibble of her burger and a long drought of the piping hot coffee and pulled out her cellphone. Maybe it would be best to call ahead this time. At this hour, her mom was probably reading her morning paper before getting ready for her factory job.

The phone rang twice and her mom answered, "Hello?"

Her voice sounded smaller, more tired than it had the last time Natalie had spoken to her, but it still carried the undeniable little smoker's rasp that had characterized Diane Rivers for as long as Natalie could remember.

Her heart gave an unexpected lurch and her eyes began to swim at the sound of her mom's voice. It had been so long.

She suppressed the sudden urge to spill her guts right away. "Hey, Mom."

"Natalie?" Her tone went up an incredulous note. "I didn't recognize the number. Did you change it again?"

"That's right. How are you?"

"Oh, I'm fine."

There was a beat of silence as she struggled to figure out where to start. "How is work?" she stalled.

"Well, work is work. But they moved Cheryl up, and I'll be taking her place. Tom says I shouldn't have to work so many hours then."

"That's good."

"No complaints from me."

Her mom's voice brightened a little. "What play are you in now?"

There it was. Time to break the news. "I'm in between plays right now, Mom. Things have been ... stressful."

"Oh yes. I'm sure having your dream career in New York City is very stressful." Her words were loaded with sarcasm.

"It's not that simple. I feel ..." Natalie choked. "I feel like this career is my whole life, and I'm missing something."

It was a weak and insufficient way to describe the gaping emptiness she'd felt deep in her gut ever since her argument with Marlowe, but at least she'd been honest about her feelings with her mom for once. Maybe, just maybe, the older woman could decipher a trace of the pain in her voice.

"Look, Natalie. That's the kind of attitude that made me miss out on my career; made me chase after your father instead of following my dreams. You saw how that turned out."

"I know, I know, Mom. I'm just … tired all of a sudden."

"Well that's part of working hard, Natalie. I don't know why you never seemed to get that. You always wanted everything handed to you."

Natalie squeezed her eyes shut. She couldn't really argue with that. Fat teardrops began to trickle through her eyelashes and sting her lids. But she swallowed down the emotion and steadied her voice. "I'm sorry Mom, but I've gotta go now. I'll talk to you later, okay?"

Natalie ended the call without waiting for a response and threw the phone into her tote bag. The tears were streaming freely now.

Every time she tried to talk to her mom about her feelings, she ended up feeling exposed and ridiculous, like she was walking the streets in the winter sleet in a spaghetti strap top.

Even when she was young, as young as she could remember, her mom had taken care of her materially, but had rarely offered maternal comfort or understanding when she was hurting. Why should this be any different?

There was no way she could go back there right now.

So now, she was right back at the beginning of her dilemma. No home and no friends.

Despite her best intentions, her mind drifted back to Kyla. She had killed and buried that relationship, and there was no possibility of reviving it unless … Her skin began to prickle, the way it usually did when she had an idea.

She'd willingly sacrificed the friendship to catch Sebastian, but they weren't together now. Maybe there was an angle there. She could tell Kyla that Sebastian had dumped Natalie because, deep down, he was still in love with Kyla. Natalie could assume the role of gracious loser and offer to help Kyla win Sebastian back.

Kyla was young and naïve—albeit a little less so, thanks to her—but still enough that she would probably buy the story.

Natalie gazed out the diner window as she continued to ponder her plan. The sun was finally coming up, as evidenced by the brighter hue that cloaked the surrounding buildings, but thanks to the lingering clouds, everything was only a different variation of gray.

All at once, exhaustion lowered over her like a heavy stage curtain. But not from hard work. Her mom was right about that. She had cheated and tricked her way into all kinds of things, but it had never been enough. And for the first time, she was just too tired to do it anymore.

Slowly, her eyes closed, and her head nodded forward.

"Hey!"

Natalie's eyes snapped open, and she shifted to face the counter. The cook was pointing a chubby finger at her. "You can't sleep here. Does this look like an Airbnb to you?"

Her eyes widened at the man's question, her mind coming to life again. She managed to conjure a smile. "Sorry about that, honey." She drew out the endearment in a deep, breathy tone, prompting his bushy eyebrows to go up.

"If you'll bring me one more cup of that incredible coffee, I'll be on my way."

With almost cartoonish haste, he grabbed the coffee pot and rushed to her table to pour. His lips curled in a grin to reveal a row of nicotine-stained teeth. But she didn't hesitate to return it. The greasy little man had given her an idea.

6

Natalie surveyed the tall, lean thirty-something man in tight fitting pants who was showing her around the apartment he was renting out on Airbnb. He smoothed a hand over his buzzed hair, calling her attention to the small golden stud that adorned his right ear.

She really wanted a few answers, but her instincts told her he wasn't the type to fall for her womanly charms. Better try a different tactic. "This place is amazing, Jaden," she gushed. "And I adore the elegant touches everywhere. Did you have a designer do all this?"

His face flushed as he raised a pale hand to his chest and tittered. "Oh, no. I threw it together myself. But thanks! I think it has a nice vibe."

"Oh, my goodness. It totally does! But come on, I am dying to know," she leaned toward him conspiratorially. "Why would you be willing to rent out such a gorgeous place so cheaply? Is there something sketchy about the building?"

He took a step back and swallowed. "Ah, well, no." Absently, he brushed a hand across his lips. "No, of course not. Does it look like a sketchy building?"

Hmm. Evasive. "No, it doesn't," she admitted. "I suppose I'll have to take my chances." She narrowed her eyes. "As to any surprises this place might be hiding … I can document them in my review."

He sighed and planted his hands on his hips. "Look, darling, you can document whatever you want on your review. But be sure to point out that you got three weeks in an East Village apartment for a steal.”

She raised what was meant to be an imposing eyebrow at him, but really didn’t have the energy to carry it off. Besides, he had a point.

Once Jaden had finished giving her keys and instructions, he hurried out the door, leaving her to explore the space alone.

It had a sunken living room with neutral-colored carpet and furnishings accented with plush, blue and yellow throw pillows. The galley-style kitchen, while small, had top-of-the-line stainless steel appliances that were more than sufficient to prepare any meal she could think of.

Passing the bathroom, she swept an admiring eye over the clean, white tile and glass shower with a luxurious rain showerhead.

It was still nearly impossible to believe her good fortune.

The diner cook’s snide remark about Airbnb had reminded her that Sebastian had once used the website to find them lodging when they’d taken a weekend trip to the Poconos. He’d talked up the benefits of staying someplace cozy, rented out by homeowners, instead of a cold, sterile hotel room.

Naturally, he had then spent the entire trip complaining about the lack of amenities. But she was nowhere near as high maintenance as he was, so before leaving the diner, she had pulled out her laptop—a gift from Sebastian—and searched Airbnb for a place to stay for a couple of weeks.

To her astonishment, amid the tiny Queens and Brooklyn rooms in her price range, there was a listing for a classy Greenwich Village apartment. She’d studied the pictures and details for a long time, trying to figure out what was wrong with it. But it was too good an opportunity to sit and ruminate over for very long, so she’d decided to jump on it.

After that, she’d gone to the closest pawnshop and sold Sebastian’s laptop for a little extra cash to cushion her budget.

Once she made it to the bedroom, she sank down onto the bed, her bones and muscles melting into the cushiony linens. It was exactly the kind of place she would have chosen for herself. What were the chances? It really was too good to be true.

Her mind roamed idly over possible explanations. Was there a leaky ceiling? A creepy maintenance guy? Once, she’d done a short run play at an experimental theater about a psychotic couple that performed bizarre science experiments on their bed-and-breakfast guests. Had she stumbled onto something like that?

Before her thoughts could settle on any more irrational speculations, she slowly drifted off into a deep sleep.

23

7

Thump. Thump. Thump.

"It's almost time for your shift, Natalie. Now hurry up and get changed."

Her mom turned away and began a rhythmic banging on the exposed pipes behind the shower wall.

"But, mom, I thought maybe I could take off work tonight. We could celebrate."

"There's no time for that. I want to get this fixed before I have to go to work. "

Thump. Thump. Thump.

Natalie woke with a jolt and sat up to look around at the bedroom she occupied alone.

What on earth?

Oh, right. The Village apartment. Now *that* was a pleasant awakening, compared to the one she was used to.

Thump. Thump. Thump.

Except for the thumping.

It sounded like a nearby neighbor was jumping on a trampoline or something.

She eased back onto her pillow and reflected on her dream. What had made her revisit that particular memory? It was odd how she could still recall it all as if it had just happened.

She had rushed home from school, glad that it was Thursday when her mom worked the night shift, since she would be home to hear Natalie's news. She arrived at the house, to find her mom in the bathroom trying to fix a bad pipe behind the shower wall.

Thump. Thump. Thump.

"Mom," Natalie called out behind her.

Thump.

"Mom!" she said louder.

Her mom finally stopped and turned. "Hey, Natalie."

"Why don't you just call a plumber to do that?"

"You mean have some Neanderthal come in here and try to charge me five hundred bucks for something I can do myself for eighty? No, thank you."

Natalie didn't argue. It was an exchange they'd had many times—really every time something went wrong with the house. Her mom went back to work.

Thump. Thump.

"Wait a minute, Mom. I need to tell you about the audition."

Her mother stopped, but didn't turn around. "You were late, weren't you?"

"Yeah, but –"

"I told you. Did they even let you try out?"

Natalie heaved an exasperated sigh. "Yes, they let me try out."

"Hm. I guess if you've got nothing else going for you, at least you inherited your father's charm."

The acid in her mom's tone made the words sound more like a slur than a compliment, but Natalie shook it off.

"Anyway, the point is, I got the part. I got the lead in the play!"

Finally, her mom turned to face her. Her expression softened with that peculiar mixture of pride and regret that some parents have when they see their children fulfill their old dreams. Then, she flashed a genuine smile. "That's great, Natalie!"

Her heart lifted at her mom's reaction. It was the quiet joy she only saw in moments like these: when she was talking about performing.

Tentatively, Natalie held out her arms and reached toward her mom, but the older woman chuckled and waved her away. "I'm a mess right now. Besides, it's almost time for your shift, Natalie. Now hurry up and get changed."

Thump. Thump. Thump.

Natalie pulled a pillow around her head to block out the present-day thumping, but she couldn't suppress the memories as easily.

Her mom had enjoyed a brief acting career in New York City before meeting her dad, a charmer who'd occupied just about every type of sales job known to man. When their short-term relationship had resulted in a long-term problem, in the form of a baby girl, they had married and moved Upstate. Five years into the marriage, her dad had split and her mom—now a single parent—had put her own acting ambitions away, once and for all.

Not surprisingly, when Natalie had shown an affinity for the stage, her mom had been pleased. The only time it was guaranteed her mom would take off work was when Natalie had a play or recital.

An affinity for the stage. For the first time in her life, she began to wonder if that was true. She groaned. Ugh! That rehearsal! How could one scene and one uptight director completely derail her?

Thump. Thump. Thump.

It was getting louder, except now it sounded more like *thump thumpty-thump. Thump thumpty-thump.* Louder and louder, as if it were approaching her door.

It was music! Specifically, it was the pumping bass of a popular hip-hop song. The name of the rapper escaped her at the moment, but he was a chart-topper. *Thump thumpty-thump.*

Now overcome with curiosity, she slid off the bed, straightening the previous day's clothing, which she'd been too tired to change out of and went to the front door.

She cracked the door open and peeked out, without removing the chain lock, but almost jumped back as the profile of a face framed with horn-rimmed glasses eclipsed the opening. The face belonged to a man, who appeared to be in his late fifties. He had to be. Nobody younger would don glasses and a sweater-vest like that. He shuffled past her door, arms loaded with a stack of pizza boxes. Beside him was a Latino teenager who was also carrying pizza boxes.

Behind them, a small, pretty teenage girl with an Afro carried a portable Bluetooth speaker. Clearly, that was the source of the music. After that, seven or eight younger boys and girls filed past, all bopping their heads and swiveling their bodies in time with the beat. The last kid in the group appeared to be eleven or twelve, and he was accompanied by a middle-aged woman—maybe the man's wife—wearing a black and tan Chanel suit.

The boy looked at the woman and gestured to her. "Come on,

Ms. D. Show us what you got!"

The rest of the kids still in Natalie's line of sight halted and turned. "Ms. D," as he had called her, didn't crack a smile, but she said, "Tryna steal my moves, little man?"

The kids all snorted and giggled.

"Hey, only if I like 'em!" he said with an elaborate shrug.

The woman began to swing her shoulders with the rhythm. The boy whooped, and the two of them danced together, accompanied by the cheers of the others.

Finally, the whole group clambered away, and the thud of a closing door reverberated down the long hall.

Natalie started to back away but paused when she heard doors start to open. She finally unhooked the chain and looked down the hall. Three doors in the hallway gaped open as various residents exited their apartments and hurried to the elevator. Oddly enough, they didn't look startled or upset by the noise. All they did was make a synchronized escape like it was a regular Saturday afternoon occurrence.

Suddenly, the cheap rent was beginning to make sense.

8

The rest of Saturday passed without any further commotion in the apartment building. In fact, things were so quiet that, by late Sunday morning, Natalie was getting stir-crazy, so she decided to find the nearest market and buy a few groceries.

She found one of those small neighborhood corner stores she loved, whose shelves boasted selections of food from all different ethnic origins. In the interest of making her money stretch, she picked out some versatile pastas and grains she could use for several meals.

On her way back to the apartment, she passed a stately church with a tall steeple that looked like it had probably been built centuries before. Despite its age, a vibrant mass of people flooded out the doors as if the service had just ended. Many of the children wore dresses and suits in bright summer colors.

One man and a teenage girl who was probably his daughter stood proudly in front of the church sign. He put his arm around her while another man took their picture with a cellphone.

Her eyes rested on the man and the girl for another minute until her heart felt an unexpected twinge. Turning, she walked down the street and away from the church.

When she was sixteen and had just started working for Betty for the first time, the kindly woman had invited her to church for Easter. It was a novelty for Natalie, so she had gone and even enjoyed it. But she'd found herself stumped by all the talk of forgiveness.

She'd told Betty, "I just don't get how Jesus could have forgiven all those people who abandoned him and even killed him. I don't even want to forgive my dad for running off when I was little."

Betty had nodded knowingly. "Is this about your dad calling and asking you to have Easter lunch with him?"

"Yeah. It's been two years since I've even heard from him, and now he thinks he can breeze into town and expect me to play *happy family?*"

Betty's smile had turned sad, but she hadn't responded.

"Look, I'm not the ultimate self-absorbed teen. I know my stuff is small compared to all that," she vaguely waved at the church they were leaving.

Betty raised a finger. "It's not small to God. Remember that. And also remember that today is about renewal and hope. Jesus forgave to give us new life and to set us an example of forgiveness. Now maybe you won't be able to accept it all at once, but I sense that there's a chance for some renewal here. Personally, I think your dad was a dodo bird for running out on you and Diane like he did. But he's still your dad, and maybe he's remembered that, too. It's worth a shot, isn't it?"

In the end, Natalie had agreed with Betty and gone to the restaurant her dad suggested, still decked in her Easter finest. She'd thought about what it would be like to have him back again while she waited.

And waited. And waited.

After an hour and a half, with no message and no sign of him, she'd finally gone home.

At her house, she'd been greeted by a note from her mom saying she'd be working an extra shift to cover for a coworker who'd wanted to be with his family for the holiday.

What a joke.

She had sat alone and sulked for all of an hour before calling her boyfriend Blair, who was willing to escape his family for some alone time with her.

Up to then, she'd kept him at a commonsense distance, but that night she'd ignored sense in favor of closeness.

A police siren wailed past, shaking her out of her memory. She looked up, startled to see she'd made her way back to the apartment without even paying attention.

Once she got off the elevator, she shuffled back to the

apartment, her footsteps sounding heavy and hollow despite the hallway carpet.

Whatever she had or hadn't done in the sixteen years since that Easter, none of it had prevented her from winding up in the same place over and over again: alone in an empty room.

She pulled out the keys, found the right one then paused as the heavy, noxious smell of smoke accosted her nostrils. Glancing around, her gaze caught on the door at the end of the hall.

Unmistakable wisps of smoke were puffing under the door.

9

Natalie dropped her groceries and hurried down the hall toward the smoking door. She placed the back of her hand against the wood and found it wasn't hot. Not yet anyway.

She slapped her palm on the door several times and yelled, "Hey, is anybody in there?"

No answer.

After knocking again, she finally tried the door handle. It gave immediately and the door swung open.

"Hey! Anybody home?"

No one seemed to be around. The entire apartment was slowly filling with a thin cloud of smoke, but it was worse in the kitchen. She coughed and covered her mouth with her sleeve, slowly making her way further inside while she searched the room.

There! A small flame was blazing on the stovetop.

She quickly scanned the kitchen and spotted an open canister of flour. Snatching it up, she rushed to the stove and sprinkled the flour over the fire until it was extinguished. Then she turned off the burner.

From the looks of things, a couple of wrappers from sticks of butter had landed on the stove burner while it was still on, and they had caught fire.

She waved her arms to clear the air, suddenly noticing the light was on inside the oven. When she opened the door, the smell of burning food seeped out, so she grabbed a potholder and pulled a tray from the oven.

The tray held three neat rows of what appeared to be lumps of coal, but were probably meant to be cookies.

She set the tray down with a thud. "Yuck."

Just then, a glass door leading from the kitchen to a back lanai swung open and the man in the horn-rimmed glasses appeared.

"Whoa!" he exclaimed, and took a step back when he saw Natalie. His eyes, already magnified by his glasses, grew even larger.

Although she needed to explain herself, for some reason, she couldn't resist taking that moment to study him better. First of all, he wasn't fifty-something after all. Up close, it was clear that he was no older than forty. But his mannerisms, glasses, thin tie, and sweater-vest conveyed an older personality.

The old dude trappings notwithstanding, he was actually tall and slim with a nice full head of dark hair cropped neatly in a schoolboy haircut.

"Is there something I can help ya with?" His words spurted out in staccato-like rhythm. He probably grew up close by—Brooklyn or New Jersey, maybe.

"Your cookies were burning," she explained flatly.

The man turned to the stove and gasped. "Aww, man! Would ya look at this mess! Why, oh why did I take time to answer that call?"

For several seconds, he continued mumbling to himself and poking at the blackened cookies, Natalie's presence all but forgotten. "Well, if you'll excuse me," she interjected, "I think I'll be going now."

She turned on her heel and navigated back toward the front door.

"Hey, hold it a minute. How'd ya know my cookies were burning?"

She faced him again to see his brow furrowed in confusion. Was the man really that oblivious? She gestured around the still smoke-filled kitchen. "The smoke! I could see and smell it all the way down the hallway. I thought the apartment was on fire!"

His eyes widened even more. "You thought the apartment was … Oh, geez. Was there a fire?"

"There was, actually. A little one on the stove, but I put it out before I got the cookies out of the oven."

"Gee, that was awfully good of you. A lot of people wouldn't have even noticed."

He wiped his hand off and stuck it out to her.

She hesitated a second, then walked over and accepted it. He closed his large fingers around her hand in a firm yet gentle grip that seemed to emanate warmth. Looking straight into her eyes, he smiled. "Thank you."

Never in her life had she met anyone who actually had a twinkle in his eye; it always sounded like something made-up. But this man's large brown eyes actually twinkled when he grinned, making his whole face seem youthful and alive.

He pumped her hand up and down. "Seriously. Thanks very much, Ms. ..."

"Rivers. My name is Natalie Rivers."

His smile broadened. "Nice to meet ya. I'm Glenn Valenti."

After a minute, she flexed her fingers, and his eyes darted down to their joined hands. "I'm sorry."

He pulled away but continued smiling. "I really am grateful."

"Don't mention it. But while we're still on the subject, do you mind my asking what this is all for?" She swept her arm over the cluttered countertops.

"Ha. It's a long story. My church recently started sponsoring a group of youth from poor—well, from economically disadvantaged areas in the city. So far, it's been a bunch of random things: school supply shopping, field trips, ya know. They come by here for pizza every other week, too. But next week, we're going to take them on a two-week camp retreat, and I thought they might like some cookies for the road. It seemed better to make them instead of buying them."

Natalie frowned. "Better how? You mean because they're poor kids, it doesn't matter if you give them subpar cookies?"

His face fell. "No. It's not that. It's just ... some of these kids don't have much of a home life. Ya know how it is: single parents, working parents, and all that. And nobody has the time to bake something just for them."

Her jaw went slack at his words. But before she could even start to formulate a response, he distracted her by hanging his head and sinking onto the kitchen barstool. "I guess it was stupid, especially when I didn't know what I was doing."

His forlorn reaction tore at her heart unexpectedly. "Hey, don't say that. I shouldn't have criticized; it's really a great idea. In fact, what if I help you remake the batch?"

His head shot up, and he slid to his feet. "Really? Are you a baker?"

"No, I'm an actor, but I know how to make cookies without killing anyone."

He blinked for a second then threw his head back and roared with laughter. "That's great!"

His mirth was cut short by a rap on the door, which was still ajar. An irate-looking man in his sixties stood in the doorway and pointed at Glenn. "This is the last straw! The entire hallway filled up with smoke! And how did you keep from setting off the smoke alarm? You didn't disable yours, did you?"

Glenn's posture drooped once again, and he trudged over to the angry man. "I'm sorry about all this, Tyson. I don't know what to tell ya except I was being an idiot and got it in my head that I was going to make cookies for the kids. Obviously, I didn't know what I was doing. I'm really sorry about that. I didn't mean to disrupt anything or cause any harm."

By now, Glenn had the look of a schoolkid who always got picked last in the PE baseball game.

Tyson nervously shifted from foot to foot. "Well—well, don't take it to heart, but please, please … try to be more careful next time. We don't need the fire department called out."

He started toward the door. "And don't worry about the others on the floor. If anybody complains, I'll deal with them, okay?"

Glenn suddenly straightened and moved to clap the man on the shoulder. "Aw, that's very decent, Tyson. You've got to be the most patient superintendent I've ever dealt with. That's why I love living here. You really care about the residents."

Tyson's face reddened at the praise. "Yeah, well I try," he mumbled. "I'll see you around." With that, he hurried from the room.

Glenn waved at the man's retreating figure, then turned to face Natalie.

She crossed her arms and tapped her fingers on her sleeve. "Well, well. That was quite the performance!"

His head jolted back. "Whaddya mean?"

She explained, "Ever since yesterday afternoon, when I looked out my door to see you and those kids parade by, I wondered how you kept from getting a dozen complaints from the other residents. And I *especially* wondered when you said this happens every other week. But now I get it! If anyone complains, you do your hangdog routine like you just did, and they feel so bad that they back off. Shoot! You even fooled me with it the first time."

She probably sounded snarky to him, but she was genuinely impressed. Nine times out of ten, the old saying held true: You can't con a con. Clearly, Glenn Valenti was the exception.

He frowned as he seemed to ponder her words, but then, that twinkle sparked to life in his eyes again. Abruptly, he tossed up his hands. "Okay. Okay. Ya got me! I have to say, Ms. Rivers, I admire your perspicacity."

Natalie raised an eyebrow at him. That was a new one.

He sat down. "I may guilt-trip the neighbors into letting me have the kids here now and then. Is that so wrong?"

"I'm hardly one to judge," she replied.

He gestured around the room. "Look at this place! Anybody that lives in this building is doing okay, just like me. It may not be Fifth Avenue, but people here are a bunch of fat cats compared to most of the world. It's not gonna kill anybody to put up with a little noise every two weeks so some kids that really need a break can have a place to hang out besides the street. Now is it?"

The warmth that had briefly wrapped around her when they first shook hands returned. "No, I suppose not," she murmured.

The front door squeaked open wide. "And that's exactly the attitude that helped him convince the executive leadership of his company to take a pay cut two years ago. Good thing, too. It helped the bottom line and boosted the company image."

This time, Natalie wasn't startled by the interruption; she was coming to expect it, really. Glancing up, she saw the woman in the Chanel suit from the day before.

"Darla! How are ya?" Glenn greeted her with a kiss to the cheek.

"Did you know your door was open?" she asked, returning his gesture with an air kiss.

"Yeah, it's been a hectic afternoon," he explained.

"So I see." Darla's amber eyes focused on Natalie, and she extended her hand. "Darla Mayhew."

"Oh, I'm sorry! I should have made the introductions," Glenn exclaimed.

Natalie shook Darla's hand. "Natalie Rivers."

"Hmm," Darla mused. "You look familiar. Have we met?"

"She's an actress," Glenn volunteered.

"Oh, okay. Were you in *Along the Path* last season?" Darla asked.

Natalie's lips parted. "Yes. I was understudy to the second lead, but I only did a few performances."

Darla nodded vigorously. "I thought so. You did a fine job, and it was a good play."

"Thanks."

Darla turned to converse with Glenn, but Natalie didn't follow the discussion.

Darla was an odd one. There was a no-nonsense kindness in her words, yet her face stayed nearly a constant neutral mask. It was as if she were reading lines for the first time without bothering to get into character yet.

"Natalie is going to help with the cookies," Glenn announced, reclaiming her attention.

Darla squinted. "But she's an actress."

"Yeah, but she's a non-homicidal baker too."

"Oh. Unlike you, you mean?"

Glenn laughed. "Exactly!"

Of all the ways she'd envisioned spending her Sunday afternoon, none of them involved baking three dozen chocolate chip cookies or teaching two complete strangers the finer points of forming the perfect cookie dough. Yet Glenn and Darla were gracious students and eccentric to the point of being entertaining. Maybe that's why she didn't even realize until she returned to her apartment that she had just devoted most of her day to helping someone without once wondering what was in it for her.

10

Natalie tossed the bowtie pasta in her homemade dressing until it was fully coated. Then she wiped her hands and turned up the volume on the Bluetooth speaker that Jaden kept in his kitchen. She swayed her hips to the sensuous tango-like cover of "Some of These Days."

And when you leave me, you know you're gonna grieve me …

She smirked at the lyrics. Since she'd more or less landed on her feet, she wasn't grieving Sebastian's absence. But then, he probably wasn't grieving hers either. The gritty truth of their relationship spread out before her like a negative play review.

With a sigh, she popped one of the coated pastas into her mouth. Mmm. Perfect. It was tangy, yet smooth, with a dash of full-bodied sweetness from the red wine vinegar.

One thing was certain: If she'd started cooking for him earlier, Sebastian would probably be begging her to come back by now. That thought brought her little glee, though, as she continued tossing her salad.

Did she actually possess any real talent beyond that of being a diner cook?

Ever since that stupid argument with Marlowe, she had been thinking over her years of acting, all the way back to her first high school play. It had been *Macbeth*. She honestly couldn't remember anything about the rehearsal or preparation. All she could recall was standing on the stage at the end of the show, taking her bow while families and school staff cheered and clapped. For a second, she had closed her eyes and savored the sound. It had felt like the first time she'd received a genuine embrace in ages.

She closed her eyes now and groaned. What had it all been about anyway? The acceptance and approval she got from being the best "faker"? That's what Marlowe had called her. What if—

Knock. Knock. Knock.

Her eyes flew open at the interruption. "Now what?" she grumbled, even though she was sort of glad to be pulled from the swirling vortex of her reflections.

She opened the door to find Glenn standing in the hall and smiling. "Got a minute?"

Her own smile emerged, wide and unforced. "Sure, come on in."

As he walked in, he seemed immediately drawn to the speaker. "Nice band. Who is it?"

"They're called the Hot Sardines."

He closed his eyes and listened, appreciatively nodding in time with the beat. "They've got good brass. You a jazz fan?"

"Yeah. The lady who ran the diner I worked in when I was young loved the old standards—everything from Fats Waller to Duke Ellington." She pointed at the speaker. "I like these guys because they take the classics and spice them up. I'd love to hear them live sometime."

Turning her back to him, she moved to adjust the volume. "Anyway. I'm sure you didn't come here to talk about music, so I'll turn this down."

"Funny ya should say that. I *am* here about the music. See, it's pretty loud. I can hear it all the way down the hall, and it's disruptive. Ya really ought to be more considerate of your neighbors."

She froze in place. *What?* Then a startled laugh bubbled up inside and threatened to burst out. But she forced it down. What a joker!

It took only half a second to get into character. Then she turned to face him. Her shoulders drooped, and she sent a guilty stare down to her shoes. "Oh, gee, Mr. Valenti," she said, her tone one of chagrin with a Jersey flair. "I'm so sorry. I'll bet ya think I'm da worst neighbor evah!"

Glenn's eyebrows shot up and he gaped at her. But then he doubled over with laughter. "Oh man, if they ever make a play based on my life, do me a favor and don't audition for the lead. Not sure my ego could handle it!"

"I won't, I promise," she assured him with a laugh. "Now what did you want to talk to me about, really?"

He wiped his eyes. "Oh, that. I was wondering if … hey, something smells good." His eyes scanned the kitchen. "Did I interrupt your dinner?"

"I was just about to start, actually. Would you like to join me?"

His face brightened at the suggestion, but soon dimmed again. "Ya better hear what I have to say first. Might want to throw me out after that."

"Okay …"

"Well, you know the camp Darla and I are going to take the kids to for a couple of weeks?"

"Yes, I remember you mentioning it yesterday."

"So we had this guy lined up to make all the food for it. He owns a restaurant, so he's really good at that kind of thing. But he called me this morning and said he caught a stomach bug, and he doesn't feel comfortable serving anything to anyone right now."

"That's too bad."

"Yeah, and we're leaving tomorrow, but now we're scrambling to find somebody to replace him." He took a deep breath. "Look, I know it's not your work now, but I remember you said you used to work in a diner when you were a kid. So I was wondering, since you're in between plays and everything … would you consider coming along to help us out? We would pay for your time, of course. It'd basically be a temporary job and you'd be doing us a big, big favor."

She took a dazed step backwards. A job? That was unexpected, but she was going to need to find something soon before her money ran out completely. Her original plan had been to go home and work at Betty's Diner, anyway. This wasn't much different. Feeding a couple dozen kids would be challenging, but nothing she couldn't handle. And the money could help her stay in the city until she either got another job, or better yet, landed a new role.

Refocusing on Glenn, she found him fidgeting with his necktie and sweater-vest, all while pretending not to watch her. "Sure, I would be glad to help out with that."

"Great! I thought you would." His grin returned in full force. "Darla said I was off my rocker to ask. She said you'd have better things to do. But I said, 'I'm sure she does have better things to do, but I'll bet she'll help us out anyway. She has a good heart; I can tell.'"

Natalie swallowed and chuckled nervously. "You can stop with the flattery now. I already agreed to do it."

He held up his hand in an appeasing gesture. "No flattery! My specialty is guilt-tripping, remember?"

"Oh, that's right. How could I forget?"

Yet he hadn't done either of those things with her. He had relied on her heart, believing she'd agree out of kindness! Yet all she'd done was think about the money. The disconnect settled in her stomach and soured there. It was the same odd feeling she'd gotten a few nights before, when thinking about how she had treated Kyla.

Clearing her throat, she did her best to ignore her discomfort. "Since I'm leaving tomorrow, I can't save this pasta salad for leftovers, so please help yourself to a plate."

He rubbed his hands together. "That's so nice. Thanks!"

They sat down and, while they ate, he provided details on the camp and kids, interspersed with frequent compliments on her food.

****

The next morning, Natalie found herself seated at the back of a small church bus that also held Glenn, Darla, and about thirty children, ages ranging from pre-adolescent to teenagers.

As the bus rumbled across bridges and highways to finally leave the city behind, brighter and brighter sunlight began to stream through the windows. It would've almost been tranquil, were it not for the nearly constant commotion caused by her traveling companions.

Leaning her head back on the seat, she closed her eyes against the cacophony of chattering, giggles, and occasional spats. It suddenly occurred to her that she hadn't given full consideration to how much she would have to be around these kids when she'd accepted the job. How shortsighted.

Still, with any luck, there would be no need to really interact with them except at mealtime, during which, the barrier of the kitchen would insulate her.

She was about to drift off to sleep when a memory overtook her.

She was in the living room of the tiny apartment she'd lived in almost fifteen years ago.

"Natalie, could you come in here, please?" a voice called from inside the bathroom.

She walked in and saw EJ tickling and making faces at the baby that sat on the bathroom counter. When he heard her enter, he turned. "Natalie, I absolutely have to see my grandmother today. If I don't go now, I won't catch her before she goes to bed. Do you think you could finish up Timmy's bath?"

"Yeah, sure. Go on."

His forehead crinkled. "Are you sure you'll be okay?"

"EJ, I think I can give my own baby a bath!" she snapped.

He flinched and held up the hand he wasn't holding the baby with. "All right, all right. I'm sure you can. I'll see you later."

It didn't take long for her to realize that she had overestimated her abilities. Timmy grew fidgety, fussy, and uncooperative as soon as EJ left, probably because he was used to getting his baths from EJ. When she finally managed to finish the bath and get the baby diapered and dressed, he randomly started wailing for no reason she could figure out.

She stared at him for a few minutes then hugged him against her, but he continued to squirm. Slowly, she went numb all over, and her chest tightened, constricting her breath.

The sensation had come over her a couple of times before when she'd held him, but she hadn't told anyone. Abruptly but gently, she pulled the baby away and put him in his crib.

He continued crying and, by the time EJ returned, she was at her wit's end.

To his credit, EJ didn't gloat over her failure. Instead, he held Timmy until the crying stopped. But he never asked her to bathe him again, and she didn't give him a chance. From then on, she kept her distance whenever possible.

"Natalie!" her eyes snapped open to see Darla standing over her.

Glenn stumbled to the back of the bus and glared at Darla. "You should've let her snooze. She's got her work cut out, ya know?"

Darla sat down next to Natalie. "We need to give her the

contract.”

With an exasperated sigh, Glenn sat down on Natalie’s other side.

Darla reached into her large shoulder bag and pulled out a piece of paper. “Here you are, Natalie. This is a low-key contract we drew up for what you’ll be doing for us in the next two weeks.”

Natalie accepted the document and began scanning it. These business types sure liked to check all their boxes.

Almost immediately, her eyes went to the paragraph about compensation, but the figure printed there almost made her drop the paper. It was more than twice what she’d anticipated.

She stared at the figure and bit her lip. These two had clearly never employed anyone in food service before. Their unfamiliarity with such matters was definitely going to benefit her. It would be best to hurry up and sign before they changed their minds.

“Everything look fair and square?” Glenn asked.

She looked at him and then at Darla. They were both perched near the edges of their seats, anxious, it seemed, to see if she was happy with the terms.

“This is too much money!” she blurted out.

Several wordless beats passed. The kids continued to chatter, and the bus continued to rattle. But the conversation had screeched to a halt.

It was a troubling mystery that she’d felt compelled to make such an outburst. The only thing resembling an explanation was a vague notion that she couldn’t bring herself to swindle these people.

After a moment, Glenn sent Darla a wink. Her only response was to shrug before returning her focus to Natalie. “We did a quick study of industry standards for this type of work and started there,” she explained.

“Right,” Glenn continued, “and then we took into consideration the opportunity cost of the work you’d be missing by helping us for two weeks.”

“W-wow. That will be great, thanks.” The trite response didn’t properly convey either her shock or appreciation, but it was all she could think to say.

After talking a few more minutes, they left her alone to finish reading the contract, but all she could do was gawk at their retreating figures.

She'd overheard enough of an earlier conversation to get the idea that Glenn and Darla were funding some of the camp themselves, including the cost of hiring her. Maybe the money they were giving her wasn't much to them, but it was a big deal to her. It would keep her going until she found more work.

It was also a big deal that they'd put so much consideration into what to pay her. They seemed to think it was fair, but it was more than that. It was generous.

She hadn't known many generous people, but she did know there were different types of them. There were those that threw money around to enjoy the tax breaks, see their names on buildings, and hear themselves called ego-boosting names like "philanthropist" or "patron of the arts." But Glenn and Darla didn't really fit that part. They seemed to throw their time around more than their money.

There was a lull in the kids' chaos just as Glenn pointed his thumb toward Natalie and leaned toward Darla. "Told ya she had a good heart, didn't I?"

Her stomach plummeted.

Then there were the people who were fair and generous with like-minded people.

She leaned her head back and cringed. Glenn and Marla thought she was like them.

Sure, they were in a different socioeconomic class, but they were also churchgoing, kind, and considerate. And somehow, she had managed to make them think she was too. What an absurd turn of events! If they only knew! She bit her lip to keep from laughing aloud, but before long, her merriment died.

If they *did* know what she was really like, they wouldn't want anything to do with her. They might even fire her. That would be just her luck!

She couldn't let that happen. She would have to make sure they didn't find out about her. If keeping this job was contingent on her kindness and good nature, then so be it!

She was an actress, after all. And this would just be another role.

11

The property where the camp was located was nestled in a verdant wooded area fifteen or twenty miles away from anything resembling a main highway. Several cabins for the kids to share were sprinkled through the trees and arranged around a clearing where a larger building stood. This housed the kitchen, dining room, several other multi-purpose rooms, and two sleeping quarters—one for Glenn and one that Darla and Natalie agreed to share.

The bus trip had been long since they'd stopped once for lunch and another time to let the kids blow off steam in a park. Once they arrived, Natalie barely had time to assess the kitchen equipment and purchase supplies before it was time for dinner. For the first night, she elected to keep things simple with tomato soup and grilled cheese.

"I thought those kids devoured pizza, but that was before I saw them with star-shaped grilled cheese sandwiches," Darla announced from the kitchen doorway.

Natalie looked up from the counter where she was collecting dozens of bread crusts. "I'm glad they liked them."

"That's a lot of leftover bread!"

"Yes, I thought I would save it to make homemade croutons for a salad bar later this week."

A subtle flicker of approval flashed through Darla's eyes. "That's very efficient."

"Thanks."

"Hey, good news, Natalie!" Glenn burst through the kitchen door, nearly crashing into Darla. "The kids are over the moon for your little stars!"

"Huh?" He elbowed Darla. "Huh? Over the moon for the stars? Get it?"

Darla rolled her eyes. She picked up the final tray of sandwiches and swiveled toward the kitchen door, but before she left, she showed Glenn her teeth. "Don't be so cheesy!"

She stalked off, accompanied by the sound of Glenn's roaring laughter. "Cheesy! That's a good one!"

Natalie chuckled at their banter. "I'm beginning to see why the kids like you guys so much."

She moved across the kitchen to pick up a large pot she had earlier filled with soapy dishwater to soak away the residue of the tomato soup.

"Hey, thank you," Glenn said. Then he saw what she was doing. "Oh! Here! Let me carry that to the sink."

Natalie stepped back and allowed him to take the pot, still trying to get used to his courtesy. Earlier, when she'd returned from the grocery store and had started unloading the supplies, Glenn had immediately appeared by her side to take the big items for her. Now he was carrying the heaviest dishes to the sink.

"You really don't have to do that," she said. "I can manage."

"I'm sure you can. But sometimes when the ladies are around, guys like to show off their muscles ... even the homely guys," he finished with a self-deprecating tap to his chest.

Natalie laughed, and reached out to brush his sleeve. "Any man who helps with the dishes is an Adonis, as far as I'm concerned."

He glanced down where her hand touched his arm for a second, then quickly looked up again. "I like that. Did you see it on a sampler somewhere?"

"No, it's something an old friend of mine used to say," she answered. It was only her first day as camp cook and she was already channeling her former employer, Betty.

After depositing another bowl in the sink, Glenn surveyed the stack of plates and pots and gasped. "Boy, would ya look at all those dishes! Just from sandwiches and soup?"

He combed his hand through his hair. "Listen, the kids are supposed to watch a movie and I gotta go set things up, but what if I send a couple of them in here to help with cleanup? It'd be good for them, I think."

"No!" Natalie replied so sharply that Glenn's jaw dropped and he took a step backwards.

She winced inwardly. *Kindness. Kindness. Kindness.*

Assuming a more relaxed pose, she leaned her elbows on the countertop. "Thank you. I really appreciate your concern, but ..."

What could she say? *I'm sorry, Glenn, but I don't really get along with kids?* That would probably sound like the polar opposite of kindness to someone like him. She needed to improvise an explanation for her objection, and fast.

Looking down at her hands, she continued. "I was raised by a single mom. She worked in the evening quite a bit and, a lot of times, I was left to get my own dinner, do my own laundry, and things like that. But sometimes I would go to Betty's. Whenever I came in, she would bring me the daily special plus a big piece of pie, and basically way more food than I could ever eat by myself. Then she'd take the dishes away to clean and leave me to mess around with the old jukebox she kept in there and ... well, I felt cared for."

Glenn moved forward and leaned on the counter across from her. She sent him a smile. "I guess I'm trying to say that the kids probably do need to learn life skills, but for now, we should just let them be kids. Just let me ..." she hedged. Let her what? Care for them? That was a laugh. "Let me take care of it," she finished.

His face was solemn and intense as he watched her. Being on the other side of his dark brown eyes when he was cheerful had been disconcerting from the first. But this was another level completely. He seemed to be gazing into her heart, as if the memories and sadness she'd just shared were playing out before him. Finally, he nodded. "You're absolutely right. I'll let you handle it."

Then he reached over and gave her hand the lightest of squeezes. "Thanks for sharing that with me."

With that, he was gone from the kitchen and off to help the kids with their movie time.

12

The secluded natural beauty of the camp, which had seemed so striking earlier that day, became less charming that night once Natalie realized there was virtually no Wi-Fi or cell phone service.

Sitting on her bed in the room she was sharing with Darla, Natalie held her phone in the air and moved it from side to side a couple of times in an attempt to get more bars, but it was futile.

"Yeah, we probably should've warned you about the terrible service out here," Darla said from across the room, where she sat writing at a desk.

A snarky rejoinder settled on the tip of her tongue, but she swallowed it back at the last minute. She was supposed to be kind, after all. Schooling her face into a pleasant expression, she said, "Well, we are pretty far away from town. I probably would have realized it would be like this, if I'd paid closer attention."

Darla stood up and went to the closet where her suitcases were stored. "I brought some books with me. Not exactly Book of the Month stuff, but you're welcome to borrow any of them."

She crossed the room to Natalie's bed holding a stack of books. "These are from a class that I will be facilitating at church next fall. Have a look."

"Thank you." Natalie made a show of examining each book's title so as not to appear ungracious. As might be expected from a church class, all the books were about the Bible and religion. She finally selected the one that had the thinnest binding and most colorful cover and thanked Darla again.

"No problem," Darla said with the easy brusqueness that Natalie was starting to get accustomed to. "Hit me up if you need another after you finish that one." She took the rest of the books and returned them to her suitcase.

Natalie flipped through her chosen book. It appeared to survey the spiritual meaning behind the so-called sacraments of church tradition—or the type of tradition that Glenn and Darla belonged to, anyway. The terminology about things like baptism and Communion would all be completely foreign to her were it not for the few times she'd visited Betty's church. In that regard, this could be interesting reading. Most of what she had seen in Betty's church had been a complete mystery to her. She could picture her old friend's shock the next time she visited her when, after reading this book, she could intelligently discuss some of the pomp and pageantry.

After delving in, she found that, despite the book's small size, it was far from an easy read. Honestly, she was gratified and a bit surprised that Darla believed her capable of comprehending it. For most of her life, Natalie's looks and personality had given many people low expectations of her intellect. That didn't bother her anymore. In fact, she had used it to her advantage on more than one occasion. But for some reason, Darla didn't seem to make any such assumptions, and it was kind of nice.

Darla couldn't know that Natalie had actually been a good student in high school, even though she'd downplayed it when it didn't seem to get her as far as her other attributes did. And even now, in her career as an actress, she often read books and watched documentaries as research for certain roles. Why should this be any different?

The book's introduction began by talking about human nature's endless longing and desires—from the most basic physical ones to deeper, emotional ones. Nothing too foreign about that. But the author's next suggestion caught her off guard: God used these endless longings as a way to eventually bring people to him.

Natalie reread that part. Looking up and, without really thinking, she said, "Darla, listen to this." Then she read the passage aloud.

While Darla absorbed the words, Natalie asked, "Do you really think that's true?"

Darla chortled, in a rare display of amusement. "I have to say I do. But, boy, is that a tough lesson to learn. I spent years fighting my way up the ladder at my company. Always thinking I'd be happy once I got another office, a larger salary—I don't know—some actual respect from my male colleagues. If only I could just get a little bit more."

She stood up from the desk, stretched, and shuffled across the room to her own bed, where she sat down and scooted until her back rested against the wall. "And I'd gotten pretty far, if I do say so myself. That's when I got one of those phone calls. You know, the ones you never seem to be ready for. The doctor saw something amiss in my blood work. After more tests, they found out I had thyroid cancer.

"I knew they'd caught it early, it has a high survival rate, and there was a clear plan of action, but it still shook me up. What if they hadn't caught it? What if it had been something worse? The whole thing made my life feel so … empty."

Darla rubbed her eyes and released a sigh. "I'd gone to church off and on out of habit for most of my life, but after all that, I started going for answers."

Natalie sat forward, intrigued. "And did you find them?"

Darla chuckled. "No, not always. Sometimes I wound up with even more questions. But what I did find was better: I found God's love. Walking in that love—or trying to, at least—completed me in a way I never thought possible."

"Wow." It was a simplistic response, but Darla's frank reminiscence had truly floored her a little.

"I guess it *is* kinda 'wow.' So was the absurd number of years I wasted before I figured it out," she added ruefully.

"But it wasn't all a waste, right? I mean, it sounds like you accomplished things. If nothing else, I'll bet you made things a little easier for the women in your company who came after you," Natalie offered.

Darla sent her an honest-to-goodness smile. "That's sweet of you to say. I hope so. At the very least, I hope they can progress without being such rhinoceroses about it, like I was."

Natalie choked. "Rhinoceroses?"

"You know: rampaging, tough skin, perpetually angry-looking."

Their ensuing laughter lightened the mood, but it didn't prevent Natalie from thinking about Darla's story long after they'd turned out the lights to go to bed.

13

The next morning, Natalie rinsed out an empty milk jug to recycle and studied the narrow vase of yellow and pale pink snapdragons that someone had placed on the kitchen windowsill. She had no idea where they'd come from, but they seemed to make the drab kitchen come alive.

The clamor of screeching chairs and chattering voices disrupted her thoughts and announced the children's arrival in the dining room. Peeking out the kitchen door, she watched as they rushed at the buffet line of scrambled eggs, sausage, and pancakes she had set out.

After Glenn and Darla managed to herd them into an orderly line, the kids swept through, piling their plates high, as if they hadn't eaten in weeks.

Natalie shook her head and returned to the kitchen for more food. They had massive appetites, as might be expected from growing kids, but this was something more. Some of them probably didn't get enough to eat at home.

Her mind drifted back to the previous night's reading and conversation with Darla. As the book had suggested, Natalie had been longing all of her life. Longing, at first, for some semblance of maternal affection. No wonder she'd always sought out Betty's perpetually welcoming nature.

Once she had gotten older and received her first tastes of masculine attention and audience appreciation, she'd craved more of both. Some mixture of all these desires, it seemed, went a long way in defining who she was now. When she thought of it like that, the image was a dismal one.

Yet it was human to desire more—even the apparently spiritually enlightened author of the book admitted that, and she thought the answer was God. Darla and Glenn clearly thought the same thing.

That was a conundrum all in itself. Maybe they were right. Maybe God had showed up for them, but if he was in the business of doing that sort of thing, Natalie had never experienced it.

Maybe He just wasn't a fan of hers. Not that she could blame him, now that she'd engaged in a little introspection. But she hadn't always been like this. She'd been innocent and young once and, even back then, "our Father in heaven" hadn't seemed any more interested in her than her earthly dad had been.

"No! I don't wanna hear it!"

Natalie jumped at the outburst and hurried to the window opening in the kitchen that allowed her to see and converse with people in the dining room.

One of the boys was standing in a corner of the room crying and flailing his arms at Glenn, who seemed to be trying to comfort him.

"It's all a bunch of—"

"Easy! Take it easy. Come here." Glenn's voice was firm but soothing as he put his hands on the boy's shoulders. Bending low, be murmured something inaudible, but whatever it was made the boy stop squirming. The shaking of his shoulders was now the only thing to indicate his lingering agitation.

"Okay, kids, we've got a lot to do. Take your trays up front, then head outside." Darla deflected the rest of the kids' attention from the scene with the calm authority of a general mustering her troops.

Eventually, they all piled up front to dispose of their trays, then bustled out the door.

Glenn continued to talk to the boy for a minute before releasing his hold and saying, "Go wash up, Kendrick, then come back out and talk to me, okay?"

Kendrick nodded and trudged away.

Glenn watched his departure and heaved a sigh. When he turned, his gaze fell on Natalie, and he sent her a sad nod.

"Is he okay?" she asked.

He approached the window where she stood. The dining room

side of the partition had tall bar stools, so he pulled one out and sat down.

"He will be, I think. It's just that his father has been in prison for a few months for a drug deal he was only barely involved in. He was supposed to get a deal for helping break up the whole thing, but it still hasn't panned out. Kendrick just found out he won't see his dad for another six months."

Glenn took off his glasses and rubbed the bridge of his nose. "Back when it first happened, I kept telling Kendrick to trust the system. Then this happened, and now he feels like ..."

"Like nothing matters anymore," Natalie finished for him.

Glenn's eyes flew open and met hers, their intensity catching her off guard even more than usual, now that the barrier of his glasses was removed. "That's right. He's frustrated because he feels so helpless. That makes two of us."

He rubbed his face again. "He's a really good kid, but I don't know how to keep encouraging him to stay that way when everything is stacked against him."

Something about seeing his despondency made her words and breath get all tangled up in her throat, and she didn't know how to improvise a good response. "I –I don't know. Maybe it's enough that there's somebody there who wants those things for him."

She almost cringed at her own banal response. If she had ever read a script with a line of dialogue like the one she'd just delivered, she probably would've ridiculed it. Yet Glenn lifted his head, and he sat up straight at her words. He seemed to latch onto her paltry encouragement like it was a firefighter's ladder, sent to deliver him from a flaming high-rise.

Something occurred to her then: he seemed so eager to encourage the kids. How often did anyone really take the time to encourage *him*?

After replacing his glasses, he sent her a crooked smile that slid through her like hot coffee. "Thanks, Natalie. You're absolutely right. I just gotta be consistent and keep being here for him through all this."

His concern for the kids showed in nearly everything he did: the way he fussed over them, and the kindness and affection in his interactions with them.

"Glenn, why do you do all of this?" she asked him abruptly. Probably too abruptly. "What I mean is, how did you get into it?"

His face grew thoughtful, and he folded his arms. "It's kind of a long story."

"Go ahead. I'll keep working." But instead of cleaning up the breakfast dishes as she'd first intended, on a whim, she went to the freezer and pulled out a container of ice cream.

Glenn began, "I had older parents. My dad was in his fifties when he had me, and my mom was just a few years behind. I was a surprise."

Natalie moved the ice cream to the sink so it could soften and so she could hide her smirk. Glenn, the surprise. That made sense.

"Then Dad died of a heart attack when I was four, and Mom passed a couple of years later," he continued. "The only other relative around was an older cousin. He wasn't too crazy about having a dumb little kid around, so he pretty well ignored me."

She flinched at that last statement, but not so much that he would notice. Sending a coy smile over her shoulder, she said, "Ignore *you*, Glenn Valenti?"

He responded with an amused grin. "Yah, it was easier back then; I was quiet. Anyway, I was feeling pretty alone and sorry for myself, and probably would have kept right on like that if it weren't for my math teacher, Mr. Perkins. He was a kind older man, pretty close to retirement age and he … well he seemed to notice what was going on with me. He'd let me come to his place and do homework, watch his old movies, and read his books."

Glenn paused, and she looked up at him from the drawer where she was searching for an ice cream scoop, but he wasn't looking at her; he appeared to be lost in the past. "It was more than that, though. He taught me things about honesty and honor. He had a lot of ideals about what a man should be: honest, fair, giving others the respect you wish you could have. I don't know what I would've done without him or who I would be."

Natalie didn't interrupt his story, even to encourage him to continue, since he didn't sound like he needed it. She located the kitchen's large blender and assembled it.

"I thought I did all the things he taught me. I grew up, studied hard, got a good job and worked my way through the corporate finance world, all while trying to be fair and honest, which ain't easy, let me tell ya! But that was basically my whole life. Then a couple of years ago, Mr. Perkins got sick. He was well into his 80s by then, so I went back home to see him."

Glenn stared down at his hands. "I'm ashamed to say it had been many years since I'd been back. When I visited, I told him all the things I'd been doing. I thought he would be proud. But for some reason, sitting there telling the man I admired most in the world all about my business success made me feel kinda hollow."

With a rueful shake of her head, Natalie scooped ice cream into the blender pitcher and returned what was left to the freezer. *Hollow.* That she could relate to.

"He died a couple of days later, and at his wake, lots of stories came out about the things he'd done for kids like me. The ones he'd given rides to school. The boy he'd taught how to tie a tie. The girl he'd taken to the father-daughter dance because her dad had been a cop killed in the line of duty … all kinds of things. It made me realize that I'd done a lot of the stuff he taught me, but I wasn't much like him. Yet I wanted to be."

Natalie added milk and chocolate sauce to the ice cream in the blender, but didn't turn the machine on yet, since she was too caught up in his story to interrupt.

"So I went to the rector of my church to talk things out. He said he figured God honored all the fairness and good behavior, but that he really shows up in love. I realized that God used Mr. Perkins to show me and all those other kids love when we needed it most. I also realized I wanted to do something like that too. So I volunteered with various charities and helped out around church until this opportunity came up. If ya wanna know the truth, I think they just asked Darla and me to help out because we were the misfits of all the other ministries. At first, I was like a zoo monkey in the pelican pen when I started trying to deal with these kids, but now that we've gotten to know each other, it's been pretty great."

"I can see that," was all she could think to say. Truthfully, it was all a little overwhelming. Fortunately, she was spared any further response by Kendrick's sudden reappearance. Glenn peeked at the boy over his shoulder and slapped the stool beside him.

While Kendrick was settling in, Natalie pressed the mix button on the blender until the ice cream mixture was smooth, then she grabbed a glass and filled it to the brim. She finished the milkshake off with a swirl of whipped cream and a cherry and set the glass in front of the boy. His tear-swollen eyes grew large. "For me?"

She nodded and gave him a wink. "Just what the doctor ordered, I think." Then she turned to clean up the kitchen.

"Ms. Natalie is a smart lady, Kendrick. She knows the way to a man's heart is through his stomach," Glenn confided in a stage whisper.

She froze for a second. Then, with slow, deliberate movements, she poured up another milkshake and garnished it. Returning to the counter, she set the glass down and slid it across the surface toward Glenn.

His gaze snapped to hers, and his eyebrows went up, but he accepted the glass. As he did, he brushed her fingertips with his own. "Thanks."

"Anytime."

She walked away to let them have their conversation, her heart and mind overloaded with the previous hour's discussion.

14

After the lunch rush, Natalie borrowed one of the several bicycles hanging around the camp and set off for a ride through the woods. She desperately needed some time alone with her thoughts, which were still reeling from her conversation with Glenn.

Growing cautiously accustomed, as she was, to his gentleness and generosity, it was hard to believe that he'd caught so many tough breaks when he was young. Like her, he'd grown up with little love. Yet he'd handled it all differently. Not only had he become a decent person, he was even able to look back at his past and see the good.

Her speeding bicycle thumped over a massive tree root, nearly jostling her from her seat, but she kept her balance like a pro.

The terrain resembled the large wooded area on the outskirts of the town she'd grown up in. She used to ride her bike through there as a shortcut to get from town to her house.

Try as she might, it was impossible for her to suppress the memory of the last time she'd ridden her bike like that. She'd just turned seventeen.

She'd pedaled furiously, branches scratching at her face and hair, hot tears rolling down her cheeks, her mom's words echoing through her pounding head.

"How could you be so stupid? And how could it take you nearly six months to figure out what was going on?"

Even in her volatile state, Natalie had been able to admit to herself that the six months bit *had* been pretty stupid. Several months before, she had misinterpreted nausea and vomiting as a stomach virus instead of the morning sickness it really was. And she had naively attributed the slight swelling in her stomach to weight gain or a metabolism issue. Maybe she'd suspected the truth, but had just been avoiding it.

Nevertheless, the truth had come out at a routine doctor's appointment. Bewildered and scared out of her mind, she'd made the mistake of telling her boyfriend Blair right away. Although he'd handled the news with more composure than Natalie had, he had also made it clear that he had no intention of ruining his family's reputation by admitting the baby was his.

Devastated and panic-stricken, she had gone home to tell her mom. Deep down, she clung to a desperate wish for comfort and understanding, but she'd been deluding herself, of course. Instead, she'd been met with fury and the repeated demand, "How could you be so stupid? Didn't you learn anything from my mistake?"

If Natalie hadn't been so distraught, she might've been amused that her mom would pose that question to her, of all people. After all, Natalie *was* the mistake, and she'd known it for almost as long as she could remember.

Her mother's reaction had ignited a painful, volatile argument that had ended with Natalie tearing out of the house in near hysterics.

Her mom was disappointed. Natalie got it. Truth be told, she was disappointed in herself. But the fact that her mom couldn't put all her expectations and judgments aside for five minutes and be a mom felt worse than a letdown. It felt like a betrayal.

After that, Natalie had gone to the only place she could think of. Even though it wasn't her day to work, she'd still wound up on a vinyl stool at the counter of Betty's Diner. Fortunately, when she arrived, there were no customers to overhear her blubbering explanation of her predicament. When she finished, Betty gave her some tea and sat down with her. She also made her hold a hot cloth over her face and breathe deeply until her shuttering sobs had subsided. Then Betty said, "I know it doesn't feel like it now, but everything is going to be okay. I promise. You're just going to have to decide what to do."

Betty's kind pragmatism had been exactly the balm needed to soothe her anguish, and they began to discuss her options.

"I can't give it away," Natalie had declared.

"Honey, think about that for a minute. The baby can go to someone who's better equipped to care for him."

But Natalie had been adamant. No, she wasn't ready to be a mother, but she couldn't just walk away, either. How would that make her any different from her dad? What would happen when the kid got older and found out his mom didn't want him? She couldn't do it.

"I don't know how, but I have to figure out a way to keep it. That's all there is to it."

"Maybe I can help."

Even after all these years—many of which had been spent trying to forget—Natalie could still remember the shock of turning around to see EJ Handler standing behind her in that diner.

EJ was a nerdy, awkward, but sweet kid her age. All through high school, he'd been one of the very few people she had ever considered a friend. She could never quite put her finger on it, but he always seemed safe. He'd never put moves on her. Never tried to use her popularity to elevate his own. In fact, he'd never even seemed to care about dumb stuff like that. Consequently, it had always felt like she could just be herself with EJ.

But that day, he had taken their friendship to another level entirely.

After sitting down with her and Betty and getting the details of her predicament beyond the ones he had walked in on, EJ offered to marry her and help raise the baby.

It had been outlandish, ill-advised, and impulsive. Betty had told him that, and he was smart enough to know it too. Natalie knew it. Yet she had accepted anyway.

At the time, she'd only been thinking of how marrying EJ could help solve her problem. When any hint of conscience flared up over the sacrifices he was willing to make, she shoved it aside—just like she did her best to shove aside the thoughts in the aftermath, too.

But today of all days, some fourteen years later, she found she couldn't ignore the memory anymore. EJ had probably been the best friend she'd ever had. Because he couldn't bear the thought of her struggling as a single mother, he had willingly taken on the responsibility of a family.

Natalie finally slowed her pedaling until she came to a clearing in the woods, where she stopped.

Bright, early afternoon sun streamed through the tree branches, dispelling the slight chill created by the shade. For a moment, she shut her eyes and breathed in the fragrance of pine.

Regardless of what had happened before or after, in that one season of her life, when she'd most desperately needed it, she had been loved. In their own particular ways, Betty and EJ had been her lifelines and she hadn't even realized it.

Was that what Glenn meant when he talked about God showing his love through other people? When people gave and protected and put their whole beings into caring for someone else, were they doing the work of God?

A robust wind began to stir around her, animating the leaves and grass and stirring the treetops. Fluffy clouds overhead rolled back like a curtain, to let a spotlight beam of sunshine illuminate the clearing where she stood.

It was like the light was glowing straight through her memories too, dispelling the shadows and revealing the possibilities.

What if God really had been present and invested in her all those years ago? What if he had sent Betty and EJ into her life to take care of her?

It was probably one of the most astonishing notions she had ever attempted to wrap her mind around, and it opened up the potential for even more. Could God have been behind other events and encounters too?

15

Natalie finished another chapter of her book and fixated on the heading of the next chapter without really seeing the words. Everything about the faith journey, as the author depicted it, seemed mysterious and complex, yet also beautiful. Especially beautiful was the narrative of Christ's redemption and continuing goodness and how it played out in the lives and worship of his followers. At some point in her life, she might have found it all pretty fanciful. But not now, because she could see it reflected in Glenn and Darla. In hindsight, she could see how Betty lived it out too.

She was also belatedly discovering that, the more she learned, the more transparent her playacting probably was. Glenn and Darla, each in their own way, were endlessly kind to her, but they surely realized she was not like them.

"Glenn seems very taken with you." Darla's abrupt observation startled Natalie from her reflections.

Her head shot up, and she twisted to face the opposite side of the room, where Darla sat on her bed, a book open on her lap. "Really?"

Darla had made the statement in true Darla fashion: abruptly with no inflection, making it nearly impossible to tell if she was angry or pleased.

"Well, he must be," Darla said. "He watches you like he's the sole spectator at a ballet where you're the prima ballerina. Not to mention getting you fresh flowers every morning like a besotted schoolboy," she finished with a shake of her head.

So the flowers had been from Glenn! She couldn't seem to stop the electric thrill that jolted her at that simple revelation. But one glance at Darla's increasingly grave expression stopped it.

Natalie cleared her throat awkwardly. "I never thought to ask before, but are you and Glenn ..."

She let the question hang in the air.

Darla looked up quickly. "Me and Glenn? Heavens, no! We never even considered it." She stroked her chin. "Well, I may have considered it once, but when I did, I came to the conclusion that the two of us would probably make a very amicable divorced couple."

Natalie snorted at the statement.

Darla continued. "That being said, he is one of my closest friends, and I want him to be happy."

Natalie's skin prickled. She sensed a warning was coming. She'd been warned away from men before—by girlfriends, yes—but also by concerned moms and sisters. Maybe it was best to meet it head-on this time. Was there a kind line for that? Something like, "Darla, I care about Glenn and I'd never want to hurt him"?

Ugh. Too trite. No, in this case, maybe kindness meant being truthful. "I don't have the best track record for making men happy. And I suspect that Glenn could be one of the few genuinely good men out there. That's why I have no intention of starting a relationship with him. You don't need to worry about that."

Darla regarded her with a frown. "I'm not worried. You're right. Glenn *is* one of the few genuinely good men out there, but most don't notice that. It would take a particular woman who'd traversed a particular set of circumstances to realize that about him. The fact that you're here and you think that, and the fact that Glenn has actually snapped out of his absentminded haze to be smitten with you ... well, it's interesting."

Natalie's heart rate picked up a beat. "Interesting how?"

"I'm thinking that maybe God brought you into each other's lives."

There it was again. Natalie leaned forward. "Glenn likes to talk about God bringing people into other people's lives, too. Do you really think that's how it works?"

"Certainly. Don't you?"

One tiny corner of her facade began to peel back. "I really don't know. I've been thinking about it a lot lately and wondering if maybe God really cared about what happened to me when I was young, and that's why he sent me friends." She paused and guffawed. "He must be pretty mad at me by now for not figuring it out sooner."

"Maybe," Darla mused. "But God has time on his side. Maybe he's just waiting for you to figure it out, and he'll keep offering until you do."

Natalie took no offense at the blunt statement, although she wasn't sure she agreed. God couldn't be offering anything. Could he? But before she could even think of voicing the denial, she stopped herself. How did she account for Glenn? For this week and this opportunity? How did she account for the no-nonsense yet kind woman talking to her now? Could it really all be God reaching out to her?

She shook her facade off a little more. "That's a nice thought, Darla, but you don't know what all I've done wrong."

"Nope. But God does. He knows about everything we've all done, but he welcomes us anyway."

Natalie mulled this over in silence for a while. Darla was so matter-of-fact about it all, as if radical forgiveness was as certain and evident as the morning sunlight. Somehow that made it more convincing.

She didn't realize how long she had been thinking until the slight rumble of Darla's snore caught her attention. She glanced in Darla's direction and chuckled. The older woman was leaning against her headboard, fast asleep.

Natalie stood up and shook Darla's shoulder. "Darla, you might want to lay down. You'll be sore if you sleep like that all night."

Darla mumbled incoherently, but settled into her bed as Natalie suggested. "Thanks, Natalie. You're a good egg," she murmured before drifting back to sleep.

Natalie suppressed a laugh and switched off the table lamp, but when she returned to her own bed, her mind was swimming too much for sleep.

A playwright she'd once worked with had told her that the words "what if?" were the most powerful ones in the world to a writer. They were exciting because they sparked original stories. But they were also terrifying because all writers questioned whether they would truly be able to bring those stories to life.

In this moment, she could relate to that paradox. What if Glenn and Darla were right? What if God had not only been good to her all this time, but he was still offering goodness? What if he was willing to take a chance on her after everything?

That wouldn't necessarily mean overlooking her mistakes; the book she'd been reading was clear on that. Repentance, new life— it was all a journey. But God directed the journey.

Yet why would he take the trouble? Here, in the darkness, she could at least admit to herself that she *hoped* he would. She hoped and even sensed that, somewhere out there in the great universe, there was a love so intense, so comprehensive, that it would make all the objects of her years of grasping and dreaming seem hollow in comparison.

Even in her imagination, it seemed wonderful to consider ... Too wonderful, maybe.

16

Pristine, rain-soaked air wafted through the open kitchen window and mingled with the delicate, heady fragrance of the lilacs on the windowsill.

Now that she knew who had brought them, Natalie's pulse fluttered each time their bright petals caught her eye. It was a reaction she did her best to attribute to simple gratitude, rather than the absurd schoolgirl bliss it more closely resembled.

The now-familiar creak of the kitchen door pulled her attention from the window, and she turned as Darla bustled inside. "Good thinking setting up that salad bar today, Natalie," she said. "That kept the kids occupied with lunch a little longer than usual."

"Thanks, Darla. I thought it might be fun for them and would help keep their minds off being cooped up inside all day because of the rain." She had chopped and arranged an array of fresh local vegetables, cheeses, and dressings, along with her house-made croutons, on a long table so the kids could create their own salad concoctions.

"Unfortunately," Darla countered with a sigh, "their minds are back on their confinement again, and they're already getting restless. That's why I was wondering, since you're finished with cleanup, do you think you could come out and help with crowd control before they start breaking stuff?"

Natalie nearly knocked over a pan she had just set in the dish drainer. "C-crowd control? You mean like … go talk to them?"

Darla stared at her, one eyebrow raised a half-inch. "That's the general idea, yes."

Natalie picked up a dishcloth to wipe her hands, but ended up wringing it and tossing it from hand to hand instead. "Maybe I shouldn't. I'm not the best with kids."

Darla grunted. "Glenn and I weren't exactly Mike and Carol Brady when we started doing this. Besides, I'm not asking you to tutor them for their ACTs, I just want you to mingle a little, so no one gets too bored."

She backed against the kitchen door and held it open for Natalie.

Natalie opened her mouth for another protest, but Darla crossed her arms and heaved an impatient sigh that made her reconsider.

Resignedly, she shuffled through the door.

Once in the dining room, Darla hurried off to referee a game of Monopoly that seemed to be getting contentious, leaving Natalie to wander among the tables alone.

Mingle a little. Mingle a little. It couldn't be that difficult. She only needed to channel the right figure … her middle school geography teacher, maybe? She'd been great with her students.

Except for the rowdy Monopoly players, most of the kids were peacefully clustered into groups, playing games or talking. But at the corner of the room, one girl was sitting by herself, just staring at the table in front of her.

Natalie remembered seeing the girl come through the meal line. She almost always had her head stuck in a book the entire time until Natalie gave her a filled plate. Then, she would lower the cover enough to send Natalie a bespectacled grin and say, "Thanks," before going right back to reading. She even read as she walked to her table.

It seemed odd that the girl wasn't reading now. A rainy afternoon would be the perfect time for getting lost in a book—not practicing transcendental meditation, or whatever she was doing now.

Curious, Natalie walked up to the girl's table and sat down. "Hey, there. You look like you're away with the pixies today."

The girl looked up, and her face contorted in confusion. "What pixies?"

Oh, right. Natalie's geography teacher had been from Australia and liked to throw around outback slang. Maybe she should've channeled someone else. She cleared her throat. "I meant you seem deep in thought."

"Oh! I'm just trying to work out something I'm writing." The girl tapped a bright purple notebook on the table.

"Something for school?"

She shook her head, making her hair bob vigorously. "No. It's something I'm doing on my own."

"Oh." Natalie studied the cover of the notebook, where the name "Licha" had been written several times in various colors of ink.

"Licha. That's a pretty name," Natalie observed.

"Thanks. I was named after my dad's mom. She was German. But my mom is from Haiti. She likes to say I'm a human melting pot."

Natalie smiled at the phrase. "And what does your dad say about that?"

Licha lowered her eyes back to the table. "He died before I was born."

Oh, dear. Of course he did. "I'm so sorry."

Licha looked up, and her face brightened. "It's okay. God's got my back."

Natalie didn't know what to do with that, so she returned her attention to the notebook. "Could I read something you've written, Licha?"

The girl's eyebrows rose high above her enormous glasses, which was an impressive feat.

Her reaction made Natalie grind her teeth. It was a no-no to ask to see a teenage girl's personal writings. She had been a teenager once; she should've known better. But to her surprise, Licha replied, "Sure," and slid the notebook across the table.

On some pages, the words were arranged into stanzas, like poetry. On others, they were formed into prose-filled paragraphs.

She stopped on one paragraph, which was a sharp but coherent invective against her school's informal caste structure. *Nice to know some things never change.* Even though at her high school, Natalie had been what most would term "popular," she'd still found the whole experience to be soul-crushing and had been eager to graduate.

After turning a few more pages, she came to the center of the notebook, which held another poem.

Natalie sat back and stared at the notebook. Finally, she looked up at the girl. "How old are you?"

"Fourteen."

"This … this is really something."

Licha edged closer and looked at the page Natalie was reading. "You really think so?"

Natalie nodded. "It's beautiful." She flipped the book closed and handed it back. "In fact, I think it's all really good."

Licha grinned. "Thanks for saying that."

Natalie returned the smile. "I'm sure your teachers say it all the time."

Licha's expression sobered. "I don't really write that much at school. My mom says I need to focus on more important stuff if I want to make it in life."

"I wouldn't say I'm winning at life right now, so maybe I'm not qualified to say, but," Natalie tapped the notebook, "this seems pretty important to me."

"Yeah! I'm writing about the stuff that's important to me—like my friends and family and God."

Licha's face came alive with enthusiasm for discussing her creative work. It seemed a shame that she didn't have the opportunity to do it more often. It felt to Natalie like Licha's talent was being squelched.

Natalie leaned back in her chair. "So what are you writing about now?"

"I'm finishing up a reflection on the Battle of Jericho."

"Hmm. I think I remember that story. Very violent."

Licha leaned forward eagerly. "Yeah, but there's more to it than that! It's about courage and faith and …" The girl looked up and over Natalie's shoulder at the sound of a scuffle. Then she rolled her eyes. "Oh, boy."

Natalie turned toward the commotion. Two of the boys who had recently been playing Uno at a nearby table were starting to push and shove one another.

Just as the fight began to escalate, a strident, blaring sound filled the room and reverberated off the walls. The boys stopped fighting and covered their ears while exclamations of annoyance and distress went up all over the room.

Licha rubbed her ear. "What was that?!"

Natalie scanned the room until she spotted Glenn. He was sitting at a corner table holding a trumpet to his mouth. He blew another note, just as loud and grating as the first. She stood up. "What on earth is that man up to now?"

Licha followed her as she walked toward Glenn. The rest of the kids slowly gathered around him too.

"Are you trying to make us go deaf?" one of the fighting boys demanded.

"Whaddya mean?" Glenn asked, eyes wide. "I'm playing music!"

"Music?" The boy replied. "That sounded like a sick elephant!"

Glenn leaned one arm on his knee. "Hey, now. Why don't ya give me a chance? See, I found this trumpet in one of the closets, and I thought I'd try it out. What's everyone else think? Think I can figure out how to play this trumpet?"

There was a collective shout of "No!" while some kids preemptively put their hands over their ears.

"Bunch of doubting Thomases, eh? We'll see about that." He noticed Natalie then, and winked, sending a rogue trickle of delight down her spine.

Then he raised the trumpet again, this time playing a scale. The kids who weren't covering their ears raised their eyebrows at one another.

He pulled back and rolled his neck from side to side before raising the instrument and playing a cheery, jazzy intro she recognized after only a few bars. She'd heard Ella Fitzgerald and Louis Armstrong croon "Cheek to Cheek" hundreds of times, probably on Betty's jukebox.

She fell back a step as he continued playing. He was good. Quite good. How did he manage to keep surprising her?

None of the kids were covering their ears now. Instead, they were all exclaiming, "No way!" and pointing at Glenn as his deft fingers depressed the valves.

More kids gathered around, and he picked up the tempo of the song. His face transformed with a frank, unadulterated exuberance that really did remind her of old pictures of Louis Armstrong playing the trumpet. His joy seemed to radiate and enfold her, bright and balmy like the first few rays of sunshine after a week of rain.

He launched into a stylized reprisal of the first verse, pressing the mouthpiece to his lips more firmly.

Ooh, he was probably a terrific kisser.

Immediately, her frame stiffened. Where in the world had that thought come from?

Glenn picked that exact moment to look straight at her, and a rare flush of embarrassment crept over her cheeks. It wasn't like he could read her thoughts, could he?

The lines around his eyes creased into a smile, just for her, it seemed, and the melody wound back to the final chorus, "Heaven, I'm in heaven, and my heart beats so that I can hardly speak …"

Her own heart was pounding fiercely as the notes echoed through her. She couldn't seem to look away from his face. What was happening to her?

His song ended then, and the kids burst into applause, snapping her to attention and causing her to realize how close she had moved to where he sat. His eyes hadn't left her yet.

"That was amazing," she murmured.

His face colored, but his grin persisted. "Thanks!"

The kids swarmed forward and began chattering, helping to fully bring her back to earth. She moved away. It was time to get back to the kitchen. Glenn obviously had the crowd control thing down.

But as she turned, she almost collided with Licha, who was still holding her purple notebook.

Her skin prickled. *The Battle of Jericho.* "I have an idea!" Natalie blurted out.

17

If someone had told Natalie a week before that she'd be organizing a children's program, for a church camp of all things, she would have laughed hysterically.

Yet here she was, having spent the last two days teaching a quartet of squirming adolescents how to sing from their diaphragms, and feeling every bit as out of place as Whoopi Goldberg's character in *Sister Act*.

The wildest part was that the whole thing had been her idea! Her vague notion that Licha ought to share her talent with her friends had morphed into a vision for a mini program that would include musical help from Glenn, along with some of the other kids.

Somehow, the plan had caught the attention of Father Reuben, the young associate rector from Glenn and Darla's church, who had stopped by the camp to see how things were going. He had been so pleased that he'd asked the kids to incorporate what they put together into a kind of church service he wanted to hold at the camp at the end of the following week.

On hearing of that development, Licha had dissolved into panic, convinced she'd never be able to present her writing in such a public setting. But after two days of coaching and tips from Natalie for managing stage fright, the girl was beginning to gain confidence.

Now they were checking out the acoustics in the small chapel where the service would be held. Natalie stood at the lectern and nodded in satisfaction. "Can you come up here, where I'm standing, Licha? I'd like you to read the Scripture to test the sound."

Licha took Natalie's place and began to read. "The Lord said to Joshua—" she paused and released a weary sigh.

"What's wrong?" Natalie asked.

"Do I really have to do all this?" The girl's glasses slid down her nose and she pushed them up again.

Natalie hesitated. Even when expressing her doubts about her ability to speak in front of the group over the past few days, Licha hadn't posed that particular question.

Stepping up beside the girl, Natalie put a tentative hand on her shoulder. "You don't *have* to do anything. Everyone will understand if you decide you can't."

Licha's whole frame relaxed.

"But I hope you will."

"Why?"

She fumbled for the right words, not just a line of dialogue, for once. "Because you have important things to say, Licha. You've got a powerful voice in there and others need to hear it."

"You really think so?"

"Absolutely."

She nodded thoughtfully, then returned her attention to the reading. "The Lord said to …" She stopped again and looked up. "Natalie, what if you did this part?"

Natalie blinked in surprise. "You want *me* to read the Scripture?"

"Yeah! It would be cool because you're an actress and …" Licha looked down at the paper she was holding, "I think I'd feel better if you were up here with me."

"O-oh." Natalie bit her lip. Did Licha really need her? No one had needed her in a long time, and the last time … well, that had been a different story. This was a simple request.

"All right, if you think it will help."

"Oh, great! Thank you!" Licha chirped, beaming her infectious grin.

18

The other kids whooped and cheered for all they were worth as Glenn and the four singers took their seats. The four of them had sung "Joshua Fit the Battle of Jericho" with impressive gusto, considering they weren't used to singing in front of people. And Glenn had provided skilled and lively accompaniment on his trumpet. Natalie was floored by the support the boys and girls gave each other.

Once the clapping stopped, she took her place at the lectern and read the text from Joshua 6, channeling her best narrator voice to draw the children into the story. It seemed to work, because when she was finished, no one was checking the clock or staring out the windows. Instead, all eyes were on her. That was a good sign for an audience so young.

Natalie reclaimed her seat next to Licha, and the girl straightened her shoulders, taking a shaky breath. When she didn't stand right away, Natalie reached over and pressed her hand, prompting her to respond with a grateful smile. Then Licha stood up straight and walked to the lectern.

"God told Joshua and his people to march around the city of Jericho for six days in a row and *seven* times on the seventh day. That seems like a weird way to work for a goal, doesn't it?" She crossed her arms and casually leaned on the lectern.

Natalie nodded in approval. *Cool and conversational. Good.* She'd watched Licha practice plenty of times, but the girl had an extemporaneous style, and her talk had changed a little with each practice such that, even now, Natalie wasn't sure exactly what Licha was going to say.

Licha continued. "Doesn't that sound kind of weird, Nikki?" She addressed one of the girls in the front row. "What if I told you God would help you make straight As, but only if you marched around the principal's desk seven times?"

Several kids snickered.

"What about you, Carlo?" She looked at a tall boy near the edge of the room. "Do you think it would help you ask a girl out if you marched around her a few times first? I mean, I'd tell you to blow a trumpet to catch the ladies, but I think that only works for Glenn."

Howls of laughter shot up all over the room, and Natalie felt her cheeks heat. Glenn's face reddened too, and he waggled a finger at Licha.

She flapped her hand at him in return. "I'm just playing. I know this story happened a long time ago. But sometimes the rules and guidelines we're supposed to follow to succeed in life today are just as confusing. The people in charge stack up all these dos and don'ts for us at school and in life and say that, if we follow them, we'll get what we want. And maybe we try. Maybe we do everything we're supposed to do and we still end up finishing last in the race. Still feeling like none of it matters." Her eyes rested on Kendrick for a moment, and she sent him a kind smile.

"But Joshua didn't hit the Israelites with some random list of guidelines. He didn't make a YouTube video called 'Josh-man's Top 7 Ways to Conquer a City.' No! This was a battle plan straight from Almighty God for how to conquer through him!

"See, from the very beginning, God had a plan for this people, to give them blessings they couldn't even imagine. Not just treasure or land; he wanted to make them his very own. Call them by his name, and set them apart as special. But they weren't always good at realizing it." She threw up her arms in frustration.

"God delivered them from slavery, and they worshipped made-up gods. God gave them miracle super food in the middle of a desert, and they whined about it. They second-guessed his goodness over and over and over."

She came out from behind the lectern and paced the floor. "But we're not much better, are we? God gives us gifts every day, like beautiful, sunny mornings, great music, friends, and people that care about us, but all we do is complain! We close our eyes. We don't notice. And we try to fill our need for God with anything else we can think of!"

Natalie swallowed hard. *Wow.* She was almost positive Licha hadn't said that last part during practice. She leaned forward, laser-focused on the girl's words.

"But God doesn't give up on us, just like He didn't give up on the Israelites. He gave them a city to conquer. Not with their own rules. But with a battle plan that reminded them who they were marching for and who they belonged to."

Licha paused and looked down for a second, as if praying or thinking. Then she looked up. "I think God has a city for every one of us. I think he has a unique plan that we couldn't dream up even if we wanted to. I think he has a bucketful of love for all of us … enough to make up for all the times and ways we thought we missed it before. And he knows there are walls keeping us from that love. Like doubts that we're not good enough for his plan or fears that we're unworthy of his love. But those aren't his walls; they're our walls! You know what? He doesn't even expect us to figure out our own way around them! He's got the battle plan to yank those walls down. All we have to do is have faith."

As Licha brought her talk to an end, Natalie scanned the room. All around, there were hopeful, encouraged expressions on the other kids' faces. Father Reuben stepped up to Licha and took her hand in both of his. "Amen! Amen, Licha. What a blessing! Thank you."

When Licha returned to her seat, she threw her arms around Natalie. "Thank you, Natalie. Thank you for helping me!"

Momentarily stunned, Natalie gaped down at the girl, but the sweetness of the gesture eventually imbued life back into her limbs. She patted her Licha's back. "You did amazing, girlfriend!"

****

Later in the evening after the service, Natalie returned to the chapel. The whole building was quiet now. All the kids had eaten dinner and gone to their rooms.

Most of the lights in the chapel had been extinguished earlier, but one remained on behind the altar, illuminating the space enough for her to find a pew and sit down. As she did, she gazed at the altar and cross and drank in the silence. But it wasn't just any silence.

God was in that space. She was sure of it.

Scooting forward, she clasped her hands and rested them on the cool wooden surface of the pew in front of her. But she didn't know where to start.

Maybe there?

"I don't know how to begin. I've done so much—made so many mistakes."

She squeezed her eyes shut and sobbed. "I've been selfish my whole life. I know it. I've been grasping for love or recognition or whatever I could get any way I could get it, when you were offering it all along. And I'm sorry."

Her head sank down to her hands as memories of her failures overpowered her thoughts. "I'm sorry. And I don't want to be this way anymore. I want to know your love if—if you can accept me. And I want to know how to give love. I'm ready for you to take down whatever walls stand between us."

For the longest time, she didn't raise her head. Would God really heed such a pathetic prayer? Her breath whooshed in and out in spasms and her temples throbbed.

Slowly, a subtle breeze wafted over her, cooling her nearly feverish forehead and playing with her hair. Was there an open window or door somewhere?

She opened her eyes and gave the room a once-over, until her attention caught on one of the stained glass windows. As best as she could make out, from her fuzzy knowledge of the Bible, the window depicted the story of the prodigal son. The son was a small figure with hunched shoulders and ragged clothes. In front of him stood the tall, bearded father, arms outstretched. Even in the dim light, she could sense the elation emanating from the father figure. How many years had she longed to have a dad that felt joy over her?

But she did.

Just like that, understanding swept through her. She was accepted! As improbable as it was, God had always loved her and he still did. He'd seen all the things she'd done and left undone, but he loved her anyway, and the gift of redemption was hers.

The knowledge filled her up until she actually thought her heart might burst with it. Once again, she closed her eyes, allowing the gratitude and amazement to overflow as tears.

19

"I can't believe tomorrow will be the last day of camp, can you?" Natalie asked Darla as she entered their room one balmy evening.

"It did seem to go by pretty fast," Darla agreed.

Natalie sat down on the side of her bed, removed her hairpins, and brushed out her hair. One thing was certain: She was going to miss those kids. She never would've believed it, but ever since the Battle of Jericho, she'd started chatting, joking around, and even playing games with them after dinner. They had apparently grown accustomed to her, in their turn, because Licha and several of the others had begged her to promise that she would come and visit them at church or at Glenn's place when they were there on a Saturday.

She was only able to tell them that she'd do her best. There would only be a few days left in her stay at the apartment when she got back, and she had no idea what she would do after that.

Glancing over at Darla, Natalie was startled to see that she wasn't reading or writing, for a change. She was staring out the room's only window, which she'd opened to let in a breeze. Maybe it was a trick of the moonlight trickling through the windblown tree branches outside, but Darla looked a little paler than usual.

"Darla, is everything all right?"

She snapped to attention and faced Natalie. "What do you mean?"

"You seem sort of distracted, I guess."

"Hmm. I think I'm a little tired. That's all. These camps take a

81

lot out of you."

Natalie nodded slowly. "I-I don't mean to pry, but I was wondering, do you still have health issues?"

Darla waved her hand dismissively. "They caught the thyroid cancer in time and took care of it. I do have to be vigilant and get regular checkups, but other than that, my health is fine."

She scooted her chair forward and pointedly asked, "What about you?"

Startled, Natalie raised her palms. "What about me?"

"I don't know… You've seemed a little different these last few days."

Natalie's lips parted. "You really think so?"

"Yes. I can't figure out what the change is, though. Contentment, maybe?"

Natalie kept quiet for a second then sprang off her bed. "Oh, Darla. I don't know how to describe it! But I do feel different. The day of the chapel service, something happened. I-I asked God to forgive me, and I believe he did! I felt his love … No, I didn't just feel it. It's like it's a part of me, it's in my skin and bones now, and everything seems different."

Excitement forced her into motion, and she paced from the closet to the window and back to her bed. "Am I making any sense at all?"

Turning to face Darla, she nearly stepped back in surprise. Her face was alight with a bright smile. "No, you're not."

"Huh?"

Darla's smile widened. "I know from my experience that it doesn't make any sense at all, but it's still true."

Natalie felt her own smile take flight. "It's still true," she murmured. Then she plopped back down on her bed. "There's so much I want to do, want to learn. Do you have any more books I can borrow?"

Darla seemed to catch the half-joking tone of Natalie's last question because her face scrunched up in amusement, but she stood and walked to the closet. "You're free to borrow from me any time, but there are two I'd like to give you."

Returning from her suitcase, she handed Natalie a small, slightly worn leather Bible. "That was one of the first ones I bought. It's a nice size for travel, and so is this."

She held out another leather-bound book. "This is a prayer

book. We use it in church, but it's also full of prayers inspired by Scripture and believers from over the centuries. In the times when I don't even know what to pray, I usually start in here."

"That's incredibly generous, Darla." Natalie held the books and caressed the covers for a second before shaking her head. "But I can't accept these."

Darla scowled. "Of course you can! I have others. And I think you'll put them to good use."

Natalie swallowed over the lump forming in her throat. "Thank you."

"You're welcome."

She sat down and flipped through the Bible, scanning verses from the Gospels about loving one another. She didn't realize she was frowning until Darla said, "Problem?"

Natalie sighed. "There is so much I want to make amends for, so many people I've hurt. I don't know where to start."

"Well, you know what they say about eating an elephant."

A sudden grin tickled the corners of her mouth. "Does it have anything to do with the corporate ladder-climbing rhinoceros you told me about last week?"

Darla narrowed her eyes at Natalie's teasing. "So? I like animal metaphors. Life can be a real jungle sometimes. Anyway, you eat an elephant a bite at a time, and maybe that's what you can do about making amends too. Address the most recent situation first, for example, whatever that may be."

"Hmmm," Natalie mused. "That's a good idea. Maybe I'll do that as soon as we get back to the city."

"Meanwhile, I want to show you something." Darla sat down beside Natalie and took the Bible. She opened to a passage that was marked and pointed.

Natalie read the verse aloud, "And all of us, with unveiled faces, seeing the glory of the Lord as though reflected in a mirror, are being transformed into the same image from one degree of glory to another; for this comes from the Lord, the Spirit."

She reread the verse to herself and looked up. "'From one degree of glory to another'? What does that mean?"

Darla smoothed the page. "I think it means that the business of transformation is a process; not a quick-change act."

"I understand *that* metaphor."

"Right." Darla patted Natalie's shoulder. "So just relax. Have joy in the process, and remember who is guiding it."

20

The day after returning to the city, Natalie made good on her promise to call Kyla. As the phone rang, her stomach felt like she'd swallowed a few dozen rocks. She'd practiced her apology several times, but she dreaded attempting to give it, since Kyla would probably disconnect the call as soon as she heard Natalie's voice. But she still had to try.

"Hi, you've reached the voicemail of Kyla Sherman. I'm sorry I missed your call, but please leave your name and contact information, and I'll get back with you as soon as possible."

"Kyla, it's Natalie. I know I'm probably the last person you want to hear from right now, but there's something I wanted to say to you. I'd rather not do it on voicemail, so could you please call me back? Thanks."

She ended the call and tossed her phone on the couch with a sigh. There was no way Kyla would actually call her back, but that was her prerogative. Kyla was under no obligation to help soothe Natalie's conscience.

For a few moments, Natalie sat and absorbed the silence of the apartment. It was an odd contrast to the noisy chaos of the camp that was taking some getting used to, but it wasn't altogether unpleasant.

Standing up, she went to the kitchen and rummaged through the cabinets until she found a teakettle. Notwithstanding the newfound sense of peace that seemed to be following her like a shadow, she realized she still needed to make a decision about her next move.

She filled the kettle with water and put it on the stove. Then she opened the tin of high-end herbal tea she'd bought at the market earlier. It was a small luxury she'd indulged in after receiving her generous stipend from Glenn and Darla.

The money would hold her over for a while. She would have liked to stay in the apartment longer, and Jaden had even messaged her to suggest it. But she would still need more work to make that happen.

A firm knock on the door suddenly resounded through the apartment.

Natalie regarded the door. Had Jaden decided to come back early?

As soon as she opened the door, her insides lit up. "Glenn! I thought you'd be at work."

"Would ya believe there was a leak in my office this morning? They had to clean and repaint the whole thing."

"What a headache! I'm sorry."

He waved his hand. "Don't be. It was time for a new paint job anyway."

"You have a knack for looking at the bright side. It's refreshing."

"Hey, thanks!"

She stepped aside. "You can come in if you want, but I'm afraid I'm not cooking anything to offer you this time. I do have tea, though."

He walked inside and leaned his elbows on the kitchen counter. "Don't have anything cooking?" He sent her an exaggerated eye roll. "Boy, if I were you, I wouldn't wanna cook anything for anyone for at least a month or two."

She giggled and leaned on the counter across from him. "Oh, I doubt it will be *that* long."

His eyes softened, and he leaned closer. "Natalie, you did such a super job with those kids."

"It wasn't too difficult preparing for that many, once I got back in the habit."

He gave his head a solemn shake. "I don't just mean the food. I mean you really took care of them and connected with them."

His praise draped over her like a pageant sash, filling her with instant confidence and pride. But those feelings faded just as quickly as they had arisen. "It was sort of a case of 'fake it till you make it.' I'm afraid connections don't come naturally to me."

He raised a skeptical brow, but didn't respond, so she pressed on. "I'm serious, Glenn. Those kids really grew on me but, normally, I … Well, I really ought to explain some things to you."

Just then, the teakettle whistled, and she turned to take it off the burner and pour. "Tea?" she asked over her shoulder.

"No, thanks. And you don't have to explain anything to me. I came over to thank you again, and to find out if you have any plans tomorrow night." He threw the last part in so quickly that she wasn't sure she had heard him correctly.

Turning to face him, she asked, "What was that?"

His face went red. "I was wondering if you'd like to go to dinner with me tomorrow night."

Her heart rate picked up. He was asking her out! "Sure, I'd love to."

"Well, I thought you'd like having someone cook for you for a change and—wait." He did a double take. "You'd love to?"

She nodded, trying to keep her grin in check.

"Well … Great! That's great! So, I'll stop by your door around 6:30 tomorrow, if that's okay."

"That will work," she assured him.

"OK, then. I'll let you get to your tea. I've got a few phone calls to make."

She walked him to the door and held it open as he exited. Then, she started to close it, but stopped short, so she could watch as he strolled down the hall back to his apartment. After he'd gone a few steps, he paused, looked up, and pointed both index fingers at the ceiling in what she could only interpret as a 'thank-you' gesture. Then he moved forward without looking down and nearly ran into his front door.

Quickly, she closed her own door before he could hear the sound of her laughter.

Back in her kitchen, she sat down at the counter and sipped her tea, but the fancy herbal leaves couldn't seem to soothe her. Her heartbeat was fluttering—actually fluttering—in anticipation of the date with Glenn.

But after a few more minutes of reflection, heavy truth settled over her. Glenn had no business dating someone like her. He couldn't know that, of course, because he'd only seen what she'd let him see. But he deserved to know everything about her.

Part of her toyed with the notion of marching down the hall right that minute, calling off the date, and telling him all about her past mistakes and attitudes right up to the point of the camp. But the other part couldn't stand to do it. Maybe she was jumping the gun. It was only one date, after all.

21

Natalie carefully applied just a smidge of lipstick. When she wasn't performing, she tended to keep her makeup subtle, but tonight, in addition to lipstick, she'd added a little eyeliner and mascara to bring out her gray-blue eyes.

After finishing her makeup, she deliberated and finally selected a sleeveless, teal A-line dress that was one of her favorites.

But her preparations couldn't distract her from the relentless concern that she wasn't doing the right thing by getting involved with Glenn.

The right thing.

How long had it been since she'd given consideration to that? For so many years, "right" had merely meant whatever was most advantageous for her. But not now. Now, she couldn't stand the thought of hurting Glenn. Even without the looming specter of her past, the odds felt stacked against her. This faith stuff was still so new to her. What if she did something stupid and messed things up? What if she broke his heart?

With a heart growing increasingly heavy, she finished dressing and went to the bedroom nightstand to pick up the Bible Darla had given her. The older woman had marked several passages in both the Bible and the prayer book, and Natalie had found them useful, both for her own questions, and for the glimpse they gave into Darla's personality.

After turning several pages, she located a passage she'd skimmed the day before and read it more carefully.

"Trust in the Lord with all your heart,
and do not rely on your own insight.
In all your ways acknowledge him,
and he will make straight your paths."

As she turned the words over in her mind, relief began to trickle through her. Maybe she didn't have to figure everything out all by herself anymore. Maybe God would care enough to help her if she cared enough to ask. So she did.

To her delight, she found a prayer for guidance in the prayer book, so she prayed the words and added the specifics of her situation, including the fear that she would hurt Glenn.

When she was finished, she felt indescribably lighter.

****

Even if she hadn't been expecting him, Natalie would have recognized Glenn's now-familiar knock on the apartment door. She opened it eagerly, but nearly swayed back when she saw him. He was dressed in a sleek, dark suit that she was almost certain was Armani, and he had slicked his thick, black hair back with gel or mousse.

She started to speak, but he stole the word she was thinking. "Whoa!" His gaze swept over her. "Natalie, you look stunning."

"Thanks. You look very nice too."

He didn't seem to hear the compliment. His eyes were fixed on her face. "You know, sometimes I forget how beautiful you are," he murmured.

"O-oh?"

"I'm sorry. That probably sounded bizarre, didn't it? I just meant …" he stopped and rubbed his chin, "when I think about you while you're not around, I think about other stuff like your kindness and talent and sense of humor. So then I see you like this tonight and … boom! I get my socks knocked off."

His words threw her into an odd limbo between tears and laughter, but the latter escaped first.

He cocked his head. "You think I'm crazy?"

"No, not at all. I honestly think that's about the nicest thing anyone has ever said to me."

"Oh, good!" He awkwardly rubbed his chin again, then exclaimed, "Oops! These are for you."

He held up a bouquet of roses. "Well, I mean … obviously, they're for you. I don't walk around toting flowers for no reason."

She laughed again as she accepted the bouquet, and this time, he joined in. "Thank you, Glenn. They're lovely."

During the taxi ride, Natalie was relieved when they reverted to their usual easygoing conversation, but she did sense an underlying excitement—for both of them.

When the car stopped, she looked out the window and realized they were at Astor Place in front of the large, red-bricked building that was once the Astor Library. Now it was the Public Theater, housing multiple theater spaces and Joe's Pub, which was a restaurant in addition to a music venue. Since Glenn had mentioned cooking when he'd asked her out, she assumed they were going there.

As he helped her exit the taxi, she said, "Live music? I'm intrigued!"

"Yah, I heard there was a good band playing at Joe's tonight." He sent her a wink. "Might say it's a *hot* band."

She chewed on his words, then abruptly came to a halt. "Wait, the Hot Sardines? Are we here to see the Hot Sardines?"

He grinned and shrugged. "I knew you were a fan so …"

A squeal of delight escaped her, and she squeezed his arm. "You're amazing!"

It was easy to see why the venue was so popular, with its excellent acoustics, cabaret ambience, and delicious cuisine. Once the band came on stage, though, it was tough to focus on any of that.

Right from the first number, the performance was everything she had anticipated and more. One of the reasons she'd always wanted to see the band live was that she knew she was only getting part of the story when she listened to the albums. But now they were experiencing all of it: the band's pure talent coupled with electric energy, the witty on-stage banter, and the rhythm of the band's tap dancer, who was like a one-man percussion section.

Every time she glanced at Glenn, he appeared to be just as thrilled with the music as she was. No doubt it was particularly enjoyable to him as a musician.

She was still reeling from Glenn's thoughtfulness. The fact that he had been observant enough to remember her favorite music and bring her here tonight was such a lovely gesture.

As she relaxed back into her seat and sipped her mocktail, the band's lead singer began her sweet, soulful rendition of the Fats Waller tune, "Keepin' Out of Mischief Now." For a second, Natalie closed her eyes and savored the tune.

I don't go for any excitement now; books are my best company,
All my opinions have changed somehow; I'm old-fashioned as can be.

She opened her eyes and felt the corners of her mouth lift. How apropos.

As strange and too-good-to-be-true as it felt, she knew in her heart she had been changed by love. God had reached out to her and gifted her with forgiveness and grace through the kids at the camp, through Darla's friendship, and through the frank generosity and regard of the man sitting beside her.

But Glenn was fast becoming so much more to her than a means to an end, no matter how wonderful that end was. He was becoming so much; in fact, she couldn't even put a name to it or fully wrap her heart around it yet.

But as the dulcet notes of the song's trombone solo stirred around her, a simple truth was stirring inside her as well: Glenn deserved to have someone care for him and, although she might be ill-equipped, she wanted that someone to be her.

Stunned by the revelation, she took a moment to study Glenn from his head all the way down to where his hand tapped the table in time to the music.

Tentatively, she lifted her right hand—startled to find it trembling a bit—and slipped it across the table underneath his.

His body jolted and he stared down at the table where they touched. But he didn't move.

Her pulse was throbbing a staccato rhythm that would've made the tap dancer jealous. Could Glenn feel it? He still wasn't moving. Had she been too forward? She had made subtle and not-so-subtle first moves on many guys before, but this felt different. Maybe she'd misunderstood his attentions. Maybe—

His strong, warm fingers closed around her hand and squeezed it then, and he shifted to give her a look so intense that it made her breath catch. Seconds or hours passed until she nearly forgot where she was.

When he finally turned to face the stage again, he wrapped her arm in his and brought their joined hands to rest against his heart.

Nope. She definitely hadn't misunderstood.

93

22

Natalie awoke Monday morning reflecting on what was probably the best weekend she had ever spent. Thinking about it energized her so much that she decided to get up and make use of the apartment building's workout room.

As she put on her exercise clothes, her eyes fell on the Metropolitan Museum of Art pamphlet that was on the dresser.

She and Glenn had decided to spend all day Saturday walking around the city, alternating between showing each other their favorite haunts, and exploring places they'd never taken the time to go before. She'd never known how captivating Manhattan could be when exploring it with someone who mattered.

Once she was dressed, she looked out the window, toying with the idea of jogging outside instead of using a treadmill. But when she saw rain droplets beading on the windowpane, she decided against it. Making her way to the workout room, she selected a treadmill and set a brisk walking pace.

It had been raining off and on since the afternoon before. On Sunday morning, she'd accepted Glenn's invitation to accompany him to church.

As she increased her pace on the treadmill, she laughed at herself for being intimidated when they'd first entered the church. The building's architecture was so large and foreboding that she'd expected the people inside to be straight-laced, formal, and aloof. But they weren't. Everyone—from the ushers, to the people seated in the pews around them, to the clergy—was courteous and

95

welcoming. The congregation was made up of people of diverse ages and nationalities, but despite their differences, they seem unified when they followed the elegant worship structure together.

Afterwards, there had been a coffee hour, where they caught up with Darla. As best as Natalie could tell, Darla was genuinely pleased to see her and even more so to see her with Glenn. Actually, that part hadn't required guessing.

"Being right is a very satisfying feeling," Darla had quipped.

After church, the three of them had an enjoyable lunch. It was nice to find that the camaraderie they had established at the camp remained intact.

Natalie picked up her pace on the treadmill again, but slowed when her phone buzzed at her. When she saw it was a text from Glenn, she laughed in surprise. She hadn't expected to hear from him much, since he'd gone out of town for work, and he didn't strike her as much of a texter.

Glenn: Good morning. I just wanted to say I'm glad I'm a lousy baker. If I hadn't almost set fire to my kitchen, I never would've met you.

Natalie: I'm glad too. But I'm thinking I probably need to teach you a few more cooking skills. I wouldn't want some other female luring you away with her baked goods.

Glenn: There couldn't be anyone like you.

Her cheeks warmed as she started to respond, but suddenly the phone started ringing and Kyla's name filled the screen.

Immediately, her stomach dropped fifty feet. She closed her eyes, took a deep breath, and answered. "Hello, Kyla."

"I got your voicemail." Kyla's tone was sharp, hard, and cautious—so different from the bubbly and good-natured lilt she'd had when they were roommates.

She hung her head and leaned on the treadmill handlebars. That change was probably her fault.

"I don't want to take up much of your time. I just have two things to say. First of all, I'm really sorry for what I did to you. You offered me genuine friendship, and I didn't appreciate it. Instead, I stabbed you in the back. You were in a relationship with Sebastian, but that didn't matter to me. I latched on to him because I thought he would make a good meal ticket. I'm ashamed to admit that, but it's true. And I'm really sorry for that."

Kyla snorted. "Why are you sorry, did he dump you or something?"

Natalie winced. She deserved that. "Yes he did, actually, but—"

"Ugh! I don't know what you want from me, Natalie, but I have to go."

"No, wait, please! I don't want anything, I swear. This is nothing more than an apology. Things have happened recently that have made me …" She was getting off track; she just needed to say her piece and let Kyla get back to her own life. "Anyway, long story short, things happened and I—I've changed, and I'm sorry."

"What? Are you trying to tell me you found God now or something?"

Natalie drew in a shaky breath. "Would you think I was nuts if I said yes?"

Kyla remained silent for a whole minute until she finally said, "What was the second thing?"

"The second thing is—and I wouldn't blame you for not wanting to listen to me of all people on this—but nothing that happened reflects on you, Kyla. Sebastian threw you over because of *me*, but you deserve better friends than that and you certainly deserve a better man. You're a thoughtful, talented woman, and you deserve good things and—and that's all I want to say. Thanks for hearing me out."

There was another long stretch of silence until Natalie had almost decided to hang up. Finally, Kyla spoke again. Her tone was softer, but still cautious. "I don't really know what to do with all of that. I guess I'll have to think about it. I didn't really mean to hear you out. I only called back because someone called the apartment a few weeks ago and left a message for you. It sounded important enough that I figured I better tell you."

"A message?"

"Yeah, she said her name was Marion Sloan, and she needed to talk to you about an urgent issue. She didn't say, but by the way she talked, I got the feeling she was some kind of cop or fed. I'll text you her number."

"Oh, okay. Thank you."

Kyla sighed. "I really do have to go now."

"I understand. Take care, Kyla."

"Goodbye."

A minute after the call ended, Kyla texted the phone number.

Natalie stared at the phone. Honestly, she could use a few minutes to process the conversation, but the phone call Kyla had mentioned sounded too important to put off.

A cop or a fed? What would someone like that want with her? True, she'd done some dishonest things when she was back home, but not really *criminal*. It seemed doubtful that any of them were significant enough to follow her now.

With a shaky sigh, she grabbed a towel and exited the workout room. Back in the apartment, she perched on a kitchen stool and punched in the number Kyla had texted her.

The phone rang twice, then a low, firm female voice answered, "This is Sloan."

"Yes, my name is Natalie Rivers. One of my former roommates told me you were trying to get in touch with me. She said it sounded serious."

"Yes. It pertains to EJ Handler."

Natalie gasped. "EJ?"

"I'm a private detective trying to help him out with a difficult situation, and I'm wondering if you might have some information that could help. Would you be willing to meet the two of us for coffee in the city tomorrow?"

Her mind was a whirl of confusion. "Well … probably so, yeah. But I don't know what help I could be. I haven't seen EJ in years."

Sloan wasn't deterred. "I appreciate your cooperation. Would ten o'clock at the espresso shop near Penn Station work?"

"That's fine."

23

Natalie had been staring at the corner of her open suitcase for several minutes, unable to bring herself to reach into the inconspicuous zipper pocket and pull out the envelope she always carried with her but hadn't opened in many years. Finally, she murmured a plea for strength and retrieved it.

She sat on the bed, opened the envelope, and pulled out the thick stack of folded papers. The first document was the certificate of her marriage to EJ, dated September 2003, and the second was a divorce decree from November 2004.

Just over a year. But the truth was, she hadn't lived with or even spoken to EJ six months prior to the divorce being finalized.

Her eyes squeezed shut and her stomach churned as she remembered one of her last conversations with EJ.

"How did this happen? How?" Hot tears were pouring down her cheeks. "He loved you more. You always acted so superior. Mr. Child Expert! How could you not see something was wrong?"

"N-Natalie, listen. I had no way of knowing," he stammered as he approached and tried to put a hand on her shoulder.

"Don't touch me!" she screamed, turning to point her finger at him. "This is on your head. It's your fault, and you'll always have to know that."

There were tears standing in EJ's eyes, and his face was pale as death itself. He simply nodded, as if he'd already accepted her words as fact.

The rustling sound of the papers falling from her lap to the floor startled her from her memory.

As she bent to pick them up again, a single tear fell on the envelope. She had blamed EJ when little Timmy had suddenly become ill and died. Back then, she hadn't been able to see anything but her own pain, but now she could see that EJ was already consumed with guilt … and grief. He had loved that baby fiercely. She couldn't imagine him being any more loving if Timmy had been his own son.

And she had added to his suffering with her blame. A sob shivered through her. Dear God, how could she? How could she?

****

Natalie gazed at the espresso shop across the street and clenched her hands. Her palms were still sweating, just as they had for nearly the entire subway ride to Penn Station.

Since the street corner where she stood was uncharacteristically free of pedestrians, she took an extra minute to pause and steady her nerves. Standing tall, she focused on taking a deep breath that expanded her diaphragm, then slowly releasing it again. She'd done it countless times before a performance, but this time, she added a simple prayer for help.

Once she was calmer, she crossed the street and entered the shop. Almost immediately, she spotted a familiar, lanky figure seated at a table near the back. As she approached, the woman he was sitting with looked up first, but he soon turned and clambered to his feet.

When their gazes met, his eyes widened. Truthfully, she was taken aback too.

In the past fourteen years, EJ's face had lost its boyish features. His tall, lean frame had filled out some, and his jaw was firmer, more determined somehow.

He held out his hand to her, slowly, carefully, as if he was uncertain whether she would take it. But she did, surprised to feel a smile warm her face. "My gosh, EJ. You look really good."

Shaking his head, he pulled out her chair for her. "So do you, Natalie. Thank you for meeting us."

He nodded toward his companion, a slender, dark-haired woman who looked to be around their same age. "This is Marion Sloan. I think you talked to her on the phone."

Right, the private investigator. As they shook hands, Sloan didn't bother to hide her cool scrutiny.

When she asked how he was, EJ caught her up on what he'd been doing, but it was hard to focus because of the underlying tension of whatever had brought the three of them together.

Finally, Sloan spoke up. "Ms. Rivers, I'll be frank with you. EJ and the friends he works with have recently been receiving threatening communications and blackmail attempts. The notes mention specific details about EJ's past that only someone well acquainted with him would know. We are here today to find out if you know … anything about that."

Sloan's eyes narrowed ever so slightly once she'd finished. She was watching for Natalie's reaction. That much was obvious, as was the *real* question behind the generic-sounding inquiry.

Turning to EJ, she asked, "You want to know if I am trying to blackmail you?"

Sloan didn't blink, but EJ squirmed and avoided her eyes.

"That would be like me, wouldn't it? Always taking, taking, taking. I guess it is sort of a habit with me. Or it was. Something has happened, though. I met someone and—things are different now."

She struggled to explain things, but it felt like she was only babbling. "I think he really cares about me. I don't think anyone's ever cared about me like that except you. I was too young and stupid to see how good you were to me back then. But now I do see. I see it with Glenn—that's his name—and it makes me want to care too. I want to try to *give* love for a change, if I can."

EJ only stared at her for a moment, but when she finally looked him in the face, a small smile lit his eyes. It was like he could hear the part of the story she wasn't telling. She'd forgotten how perceptive he could be. "Wow," he murmured. "I'm really happy for you, Natalie."

"So you live in the city now?" Sloan cut in, her expression still serious and suspicious.

Natalie didn't recoil. "Yes, I've been living here for the last few months. And you don't have to believe any of this, Ms. Sloan. You can keep looking into it, if you want, but it will be a waste of time. You'll see that I had nothing to do with the blackmail. And I don't know anything about it."

She returned her attention to EJ. "I'm glad to see you now, EJ, because I've been wanting to tell you something. I don't blame you for anything that happened all those years ago. I know I did back then, and I'm sorry for that. You're a wonderful person, and you always have been."

It seemed to take him a minute to absorb her words, but once he had, he suddenly leaned close and kissed her cheek. She closed her eyes and savored the grace of the gesture. Then, returning the kiss, she whispered, "Take care of yourself, honey."

24

After she left the espresso shop, Natalie headed up Seventh Avenue. The day was sunny and mild, and she really needed to walk. Cars whizzed by and people bustled around her, but her thoughts were too distracting to allow her to hurry.

Even if she'd bothered to speculate on what it would be like to see EJ again after so many years, she never would have imagined the scenario of being interrogated for blackmailing him.

Her heart ached for his situation. He didn't deserve it. But something about the investigator's air of determination inspired her confidence that the issue would be resolved soon.

Despite the circumstances, she was grateful for the visit and the opportunity to apologize to EJ. It had felt inadequate, but she knew he'd forgiven her nonetheless.

Her steps slowed as the full, spicy scent of roasting lamb captured her senses. Glancing around, she was surprised to spot a well-known halal food cart. She'd been so lost in her thoughts that she hadn't even realized she'd made it to 40th Street already.

Several blocks ahead, she could see the swarm of tourists wandering around Times Square. Normally, she would delve into the crowd just so she could take in the lights and show posters that had beckoned to her ever since she was a girl. But today, the prospect was exhausting. Instead, she turned and headed for Bryant Park.

After roaming the park for a few minutes, she found a grassy, unpopulated corner. Removing her sweater, she spread it out on the ground and sat down.

When she'd moved to Manhattan, she had soon learned how productive it could be, as an actor, to people-watch in a crowded park. Growing up in a small town had only afforded a limited range of people to observe. But one afternoon in the park here was like a pageant of diversity. She could study every type of personality imaginable.

Today, inevitably perhaps, her eyes fell on a young mother who sat on the grass a few yards away, bouncing her baby girl on her lap. The woman was grinning and seemed to be carrying on a full conversation with her daughter, who was squealing and giggling in return.

A dull ache settled in her stomach, and she turned away. Reaching inside her shoulder bag, she pulled out the white envelope she had put there earlier. This time, she skipped over the marriage documents and pulled out Timmy's birth certificate. As she unfolded it, a small photo fell out onto the grass.

She picked it up and dusted it off. It was a picture of Timmy when he was three months old. He was sprawled on his favorite blanket and beaming up at the camera.

Gently, she brushed the image with her fingertips. "Sweet, sweet baby." All at once, her eyes began to burn and her face crumpled. She covered her face as tears started flowing. "Oh, Timmy!"

****

Natalie managed to pull it together enough to get back to the apartment. But once she did, she threw herself on the bed and wept like she hadn't in all of her thirty-three years.

Image after image filled her mind with stunning clarity: Timmy's little pink face when the doctor first placed him into her arms, the tranquil rise and fall of his chest as he slept in his crib, his grin as he squealed when EJ held him up in the air. She had kept the mental pictures locked firmly away for so long, but now they overwhelmed her thoughts in an unstoppable flood.

Why now?

Fourteen years before, she had rushed to the hospital when EJ had called to say Timmy was seriously ill. But she'd arrived too late. That night, she had been shocked and angry. Oh, she'd cried some in the following weeks, but mostly she had been just as sickeningly numb as she had been through most of her motherhood. But now, she was drowning in grief as though it had all just happened.

For three days, she holed up in the apartment, sleeping some but hardly eating. The only outside interaction she had was several text messages from Glenn, which she managed to respond to as if nothing were wrong.

Then on the fourth night, he called.

For a second, she considered not answering. But the longing to hear his voice overpowered her hesitation.

She looked at her reflection in the mirror across from the bed and affected a full, lighthearted smile. It was a smile she would have felt from head to toe if she'd received the call a few days ago, before her heart had been wrung out like a dirty dishrag.

Finally, she answered. "Glenn, how is Boston?"

He scoffed. "The part I can see from the conference room windows seems nice."

"Ha. Sounds lovely. What about after work? Have you had a chance to do some sightseeing or go out to dinner?"

"Nah. I just eat at the hotel. Use the spare time to get paperwork ready for the next day. Guess I keep up the same habits no matter what city I'm in." His laugh was a little forced, like he was drained from the day's work.

"Glenn, there is such a thing as burnout, you know? Maybe you should think about putting the work aside and resting tonight. You would probably feel better."

He was silent for several seconds until she chuckled awkwardly. "I'm sorry. You don't need me to badger you. I was just …"

"No, no. You don't have to apologize." His voice grew softer. "I-it's nice. I haven't had many people around lately who've cared enough to badger me."

Her heart clenched unexpectedly, and a heavy curtain of despair slowly closed in front of her.

All at once, she couldn't absorb his words beyond the surface level. She heard, responded, and played at small talk, then escaped the conversation as quickly as she could.

As soon as Glenn said goodnight, she turned her phone off and threw it down on the bed. Rubbing her forehead, she tried to determine what was wrong with her now. She had made Glenn feel cared for. Wasn't that good?

I want to try to give love for a change.

Her own words seemed to mock her now. How many chances did she expect God to give her?

Years ago, he had given her a beautiful, perfect baby, and she'd been unable to muster enough maternal affection to care for him. The night he'd died, she hadn't been around. If Timmy's death had been anyone's fault, it had been hers for neglecting him.

Then there was EJ. He'd been amazing. She'd been given the chance to be a loving partner to him, and she had ignored that too.

And now she expected another chance? Did she honestly believe God would entrust her with a man like Glenn?

What had she done to deserve that?

25

Natalie made her way through the apartment one final time to ensure she wasn't leaving any of her things behind. She was moving out two days earlier than planned, but Jaden probably wouldn't care since she'd paid the full amount and had arranged to leave the key with the building staff. There was no need to leave with a guilty conscience on his account.

If only that was all she had to worry about! Reaching inside her sweater pocket, Natalie fingered the small envelope she planned to slide under Glenn's front door before she left. It was a low move, but she couldn't bear the thought of playing a scene out face-to-face.

She would go home and leave Glenn alone. It was for his own good. But she'd never be able to make him understand that.

Once she made her way back to the front of the apartment, she picked up her bags, squared her shoulders, and opened the front door.

"Hi!" Glenn stood on the other side, beaming at her. "You saved me a knock!"

She took a step back. "I thought you were coming back tomorrow." How did he always catch her by surprise?

"Negotiations finished early, so I split. How are y—" He halted and looked down. "Hey, you're packed. What's going on?"

Her stomach started to churn. "Glenn, I have to go. I need to go home."

His face crinkled in worry. "Oh, no. Is something wrong? Your family okay?"

She cringed. That's not how she meant it to sound. "Everything is fine. It's not that. It's just ..." She struggled to remember the vague explanation she'd written in the note, but the words fled her mind, especially as he moved closer and placed a firm, comforting hand on her arm.

"Please tell me what's wrong, sweetheart."

Sweetheart. It was the first endearment he'd ever used with her. Just a few days ago, it would have made her heart soar. But now she wanted to crawl into a hole and hide.

Forget the note. It was best to tell him the truth. "Okay, I'll tell you. It all started a few days ago, when I ran into someone from my past. Someone who once meant a lot to me."

She paused, trying to decide how best to get on with it, when he startled her by saying, "This someone is a man, I take it?"

Natalie met his eyes, which were now crinkled in a pained grimace as if he were preparing to swallow a bitter tonic.

"Uh, yes, it is a man, but ..." Something stopped her. Maybe it would be easier this way. No need to drag him through her sordid past until he was forced to see how wrong they really were for each other. Maybe it was best to get it over with fast and then walk away.

She swallowed hard and chose her words carefully. "Seeing him again affected me more deeply than I ever could have imagined. It made me think about a lot of things ... including us." She gestured vaguely between them and released a sigh. "I'm sorry, Glenn. I really don't think this is gonna work."

His big brown eyes searched hers carefully, and for a second, she spied a spark of rebellion. But it fizzled out as quickly as it had come. His gaze lowered, and his shoulders sank—not with the exaggerated remorse he had used back when the landlord scolded him—but with genuine resignation.

It was almost like he'd been expecting this. Her stomach roiled and swished some more.

Finally, he spoke. "You don't have to be sorry. I understand, and I want you to be happy." He ran his fingers through his hair distractedly. "This man you're talking about, he's a good man?"

A dry, hollow chuckle escaped her lips. "He's an angel," she murmured. And the cold truth remained that a woman like her couldn't ask for two of those in one lifetime.

He nodded grimly. "That's good. Thanks for being straight with me."

Everything inside her squirmed, but years of practice allowed her to keep her face a perfect mask as she said, "Thank you for understanding."

Whatever he said after that was drowned out by a sudden, intense throbbing in her head.

The moment he left, she ran to the bathroom and vomited.

26

Natalie swept her eyes over the small Cape Cod-style house that had been her home through her junior high and high school years, not to mention the few times she'd come back when money got too tight for her in Manhattan. Paint was chipping in a few places and the lawn was a little overgrown. Her mom's old green station wagon was getting faded, but overall, everything looked like it always had.

Even though she had a key, Natalie knocked. She didn't want to startle her mom by waltzing into the front door after three or four months of being away.

When the door opened, her mom stood on the threshold, eyes wide. "Natalie! What on earth?"

So much for not startling her. "Hey, Mom. I thought I'd come home for a visit."

Her mom regarded her bemusedly for a few seconds, then sighed and ran a hand over the long graying curls she had pulled back in a low ponytail. "Well, don't just stand there. Come on inside."

As Natalie followed her down the hall to the living room, her mom asked over her shoulder, "So how many bridges did you burn this time?"

Natalie glared. *Nice to see you too, Mom.* Bile rose in her throat, but she swallowed it down. "It's nothing like that, really. There's just—there's just been a lot that's happened recently, and I need some time to process. You know?"

111

Her mom turned, her face set in a bewildered frown, as if Natalie had said something bizarre. "Process? What could you possibly have to process that's worth neglecting your career for?"

"Lots of things, Mom. Like …" she struggled to explain, but her confidence waned in the face of her mom's challenge.

Her mom rolled her eyes, and shuffled into the living room.

Natalie's frustration inflated like a balloon, but it deflated when she got her first look at the living room. There were stacks of cardboard boxes everywhere, barely leaving a path to the sofa and recliner.

As they sat down, Natalie gestured around the room. "What is all of this?"

"I wanted to get the stuff we had stored in the attic organized. I told you that," her mother snapped.

Natalie ran her finger over the layer of dust covering the box closest to her. "Yeah, but that was a year ago. Haven't you made any progress since then?"

Only then did she notice that the lines around her mom's gray-blue eyes were deeper than they had been the last time she'd seen her. Her shoulders sagged a little bit too. "Mom, are you okay?"

"Of course, I'm okay. Things have just been busy at work for a while and I haven't had a chance to tackle the project yet. It's not that pressing, anyway. All I was going to do was throw out the stuff that's trash, and combine some of the boxes."

"I see."

An uncomfortable silence hung over them, so she occupied her mind with reading the labels made in faded marker on the sides of the boxes. Finally, she stood, removed her sweater, and tossed it on the sofa. "I might as well make myself useful while I'm here."

Her mom's eyes widened. "O-okay. If you want to, that would be fine. Thanks." She looked at the wall clock. "I'd like to help, but I have to get ready for work. I'm working today."

Natalie waved her hand. "Don't worry about it."

Once her mom left the room to get ready, Natalie picked a box from the top of one stack and opened it. Immediately, the musty smell of mildew greeted her. *Ew.* This one was full of old clothes. She picked up a striped blouse from the top and shook it out. It was riddled with rips and tears from where moths had snacked on it.

She took the other garments out, piece by piece, and found they were all in the same condition as the first blouse. Shaking her head, she returned the clothes to the box. *That's one box for the garbage.*

"Natalie, I have to go now," her mom called from the doorway. "I think there's some leftover Chinese food in the fridge, if you get hungry."

"Mom, wait. What time are you getting off?"

"Not until six."

"A full day on a Saturday? I thought you said you were working less."

Her mom folded her arms. "Look, I had no idea you'd be coming today, and I needed to cover for someone. If you'd called ahead, I could have made different arrangements." She glanced at her watch and headed for the door. "Now, I really have to go. We can talk later, okay?"

Without waiting for a reply, she swept out the door and shut it behind her.

Natalie stared at the closed door for a moment, the heavy silence closing in around her.

She shivered. Just like old times.

Returning to the living room, she shoved the clothing box to one side of the room to allocate for trash, and opened the next box in the stack. But she couldn't focus on the contents. Her mind kept returning to her brief interactions with her mom, especially her expression when Natalie had said she needed to process. She'd received a similar response from her mom over the years whenever she said or did something her mom considered nonsensical.

Was it too much to ask that, just once, the response would be compassion or an attempt to understand her daughter's perspective?

She blinked and tried to refocus on the box; it was filled with bundles of paperwork that appeared old enough to be past their usefulness. But she would check to make sure no official documents were mixed up with them. Her mom probably had the most important things, like birth certificates and deeds, stored somewhere else, just like Natalie did.

A sudden thought struck her with crippling force: Did her mom feel numb and disconnected whenever she witnessed one of Natalie's near breakdowns—just like Natalie had felt when trying to care for the baby? Was there a connection between them? Some missing piece within them that made sympathizing with their own children impossible?

The idea left her cold and clammy.

114

27

After another hour or so alone with her thoughts, sorting and shredding old paperwork, Natalie decided it was time for a break away from the empty house. And there was only one place she could think to go.

Her mom had kept the ancient Volkswagen Bug Natalie had bought for a song during one of her extended visits back home, but as might be expected, the battery was dead by now.

However, all she needed to do was lubricate the chains and air up the tires to make her old bicycle ready to ride again.

The terrain of the woods near her mom's house was more rugged than she remembered. It was much bumpier than the area she'd biked through at camp a few weeks before. It only took a few minutes for her body to remind her she wasn't seventeen anymore, but she managed to huff and pedal her way to Betty's Diner nonetheless.

Once she arrived, she checked her watch. It was 12:45. Since Betty closed down at noon on Saturdays, the customers would be gone but she'd still be cleaning up. She rode to the back of the diner and parked in the alley.

As soon as she walked through the back door and into the kitchen, the smell of bacon grease and pastry crust enveloped her. She shuffled through the kitchen, noting how every fixture and surface looked exactly as it always had, ever since she was a teenager.

When she got to the swinging door leading to the front of the

115

restaurant, she peaked through its porthole-style window. Betty stood on the other side, wiping down the front counter with her back to Natalie.

She pushed through the door. "Hello, Betty."

Betty started and whirled around, her face crinkled in a scowl, as if annoyed by the abrupt interruption. But as soon as she reached up to refocus her glasses, a wide grin broke out on her face. "Natalie!"

She tossed her rag down, and hurried over. "Let's have a look at you."

Sweeping her eyes up and down, she shook her head. "Tsk. Tsk. Still an Amazon, I see. Bend down here!"

Natalie choked out a laugh. "Oh, Betty." She leaned down and let Betty, who stood a good six inches shorter, wrap her in a fierce bear hug.

She squeezed her eyes against the sudden sting of tears and closed her arms around Betty. Dear Lord, what would she have ever done without this woman?

Once Betty released her, the older woman studied her face with a furrowed brow. "You look … I don't know. Sorta different."

Her furrowed brow deepened into a mock glare. "Of course, it's been forever since you've been back!"

"It's only been a few months."

"That's what I said. Anyway, you could've at least called! I never know if you're out there starring in a play, or if you've run off and joined a hippie commune or something."

"It's been a little bit of both, really," Natalie quipped.

"I'm not surprised!" Betty gestured at a booth. "Sit down, and tell me all about it. Are you hungry?"

Natalie slid into the booth. "Not really, no."

"I'll just bring you some pie then."

She disappeared into the kitchen, and Natalie chuckled. Betty had a personal ordinance that no one came into her diner without eating.

When Betty returned with two slices of her legendary grape pie and two cups of rich, steaming coffee, they enjoyed them together while Natalie recounted recent events, starting with the play and the rehearsal.

Betty listened sympathetically to the explanation of her failure, the confrontation with Marlowe, and even the breakup with

Sebastian.

She described the apartment and her first meeting with Glenn and Darla. Then in one long, messy monologue, she described her time at the camp, and those two or three glorious days right afterward.

When she was finished, she gazed down at her now tepid coffee and absently swished the cup until the traces of creamer swirled. Surprised at Betty's extended silence, she looked up to find that the woman actually had tears in her eyes. She'd never seen her cry before.

"My goodness," Betty murmured. "I prayed this would happen someday."

Natalie swallowed hard. "Prayed what would happen, exactly?"

Betty leaned forward and beamed. "That someday you would come to realize how much God loves you ... that you'd really let that love sink in, wrap around you, and transform you." Reaching over, she patted Natalie's hand. "And it has, hasn't it?"

Natalie met her old friend's eyes, longing to affirm the hope she saw there, but she had to settle for honesty. "Betty, I really don't know what's happened. I do feel different, but transformation? Maybe it only goes so far."

Shakily, she picked up her coffee cup and drained its contents, heedless of its temperature. "Two days after that first date with Glenn, something happened. I saw EJ again."

"You did?" Betty's eyes grew wide, and she sank back into her seat to listen to the rest of the story.

It was simple enough to tell about the meeting with EJ, but she struggled to explain all the feelings that had followed. Feelings about how she'd treated EJ and ... feelings about Timmy. Before she knew it, she was the one crying. "I don't know what's wrong with me, Betty. I wept for my little boy like I never once did when I lost him."

She ran her fingers through her hair. "Oh, I did cry some back then. You remember that. But I don't even know who I was crying for the most ... the baby or myself. But I cried for Timmy this time. I must've relived a hundred memories from his life in just a couple of days. And I cried for everything I'd thrown away. I cried because ..." she hesitated and threw up one hand, "because I'm ashamed of myself too, I guess. I can't understand it. Why, after so many years? How could it take this much time for me to feel, *really* feel what happened? What's wrong with me?"

Betty's face was pensive as she spoke. "Maybe it was just the right time for this. You know, when Timmy died, you pretty well made a break for it. You stuck around long enough for the divorce, but then you ran. And you've been running ever since, without giving yourself a chance to grieve or even think about what happened. But, sweetie, you can't run forever. At some point, that process just has to happen."

Natalie stared down at her empty cup. Betty had a point. Why did it sound so sensible when she said it?

"While you're chewing on that, here's something else." Betty stretched, stood up, and then shuffled to the counter. She flicked a few buttons on the coffee maker.

"Yes?" Natalie prompted.

Betty frowned at her over her glasses. "Wait a minute, I need some more coffee."

"Sorry." tapped her fingers on the table while Betty refilled both of their mugs.

When Betty sat down again, she took a sip and continued. "One of my favorite Bible verses is from the book of Ezekiel: 'A new heart I will give you, and a new spirit I will put within you; and I will remove from your body the heart of stone and give you a heart of flesh.'"

Natalie had been raising her mug to her lips when Betty started speaking, but now her hand paused midair as the words echoed through her mind. Her pulse quickened. A new heart …

Betty closed both hands around her cup and scooted close to the table. "Maybe part of the reason *this* was the right time for you to start dealing with everything is because God has been preparing your heart. Maybe he was softening and renewing it, so you can deal with your past and move ahead into the future he has in mind for you."

Natalie looked off into space as she pondered. That old, nagging, too-good-to-be-true feeling started to rear its head.

"This is probably going to be one of those concepts that will take you a few tries to get. Sort of like making omelets," Betty predicted wryly.

Natalie's thoughts scattered at the sudden memory of her first failed attempts at making omelets back when she'd first started cooking. She crinkled her nose. "This is *nothing* like making omelets."

Betty laughed. "It's not so different. You got the hang of things then, and you'll get it now." She started to raise her cup then set it back down with a clink. "But I *am* a little miffed at you."

"For what?"

"For leaving Glenn in the lurch like you did! He sounds like a really nice man."

"He *is* a nice man. That's why I thought it was best to let him off like I did: with a sensible story instead of dragging him through all the ugliness of my past."

"You mean you didn't have the gumption to tell him about your past."

Natalie winced. "Maybe not. But there's more to it than that. I care about Glenn so much, and I know that he deserves more than somebody like me."

"Somebody like you," Betty mused. Then she leaned forward. "The Natalie I know used people. She didn't care anything about the men she was in a relationship with beyond what she could get out of them."

Natalie squeezed her eyes shut, and her head dropped.

"Now, listen!" Betty bent her head low next to Natalie's. "I knew that Natalie all her life, and I loved her like she was my own."

A strangled sob escaped Natalie's throat.

"Sweetie, look at me," Betty ordered. So she did.

Betty's eyes were misty again as she murmured, "That is not the same Natalie who walked in my door today."

28

When Natalie arrived back at the house, she was surprised to realize that only a couple of hours had passed since she'd left. It felt like she'd been at Betty's for ages.

As she made her way down the hall to her old bedroom, a dozen thoughts swarmed through her head from the conversation at the diner. But the one that kept pushing its way to the foreground was Glenn, and the way she had ended things with him. Yes, once upon a time, she would've said or done anything to cut someone loose once she was ready, but that's not who she was now. And even if it cost her what little good opinion she might have left in his eyes, she needed to tell him the truth.

She sat down at her desk, located some notepaper, and began to write.

Glenn,

I owe you an apology. When I implied I wanted to end our relationship because of another man, I deceived you. The truth is I had come to terms with the fact that we aren't right for each other, but I didn't have the courage to tell you why.

Her eyes seemed to close of their own accord. "Please, help me do this," she murmured.

Then she took a deep breath and leaned back over her paper. She wrote down all the ugly details about herself and her past.

121

She recounted her marriage and divorce, the baby, and her failure as a mother. She even touched on her behavior in recent years. She spread it all out as if she were a prosecutor building a case against herself.

But, just as she had with Betty, she also attempted to explain what had happened to her at camp. It was important that Glenn knew that too.

To make a long story short, I pretended to be a better person than I really was when I first started helping you because it seemed advantageous at the time. But somewhere along the way, I really did change. I believe God changed my heart. And I will always be grateful to Darla and the children, and most especially to you for the part you played in that process.

I still don't know what I am doing with all this, and I know I have a very long way to go. You deserve more than that. You deserve someone who is already wonderful, because you are a wonderful man.

I'll never understand how your cousin could ignore you. If I had you in my life, I wouldn't want to miss a single moment.

Please take care of yourself.

Natalie

She reread her work and sealed the letter. Before she could think better of it, she hurried down the street to the nearest mailbox and stuck the letter in the slot for Monday's first pickup.

Part of her was at peace about writing the letter, but another part was twisted in knots at the prospect of Glenn learning about the real her.

It was hard not to torture herself with visions of his stunned or even horrified reaction, but she knew she had to try to leave it all in God's hands. The best thing she could do was keep her mind occupied with other things.

Once she was back in the living room, she sat down on the floor in front of the sofa and delved into another box. The cardboard was more frayed and brittle than the other boxes had been, and she made a mental note to buy some plastic storage containers that would preserve the contents better.

The first thing she found in the box was a dark brown teddy bear with the stuffing falling out. Then there was a stack of magazines that appeared to be from the early eighties. This was obviously her mom's old stuff.

As she dug further, she found a large navy yearbook. From the date, she calculated it must have been from her mom's senior year. She flipped through the pages, giggling at the crimps, perms, and mullets on every page.

She paused on a page featuring the drama club. Right in the middle on one side was a picture of her mom. She stood on a stage wearing a long, flowing Elizabethan-style costume.

Natalie marveled. Even from a still photo, it was clear that her mom had possessed an engaging stage presence. She was beautiful, tall, and graceful.

Why had she never shown Natalie any of this stuff?

"Right," she snorted. Like her mom, of all people, would sit down to share memories with her like they were in some kind of Norman Rockwell painting. When had she ever shared anything about herself?

After several moments of stewing, she finally shook off her irritation. She really needed to stop with the bitter routine. Returning her attention to the yearbook, she studied pictures until she came to the back. Dozens of faded signatures and well wishes cluttered the inside cover.

Her attention caught on one large, sprawling inscription:

Diane,

You are the most talented student I've ever taught. Congratulations on your theater scholarship. I know we'll see great things from you someday.

Mr. Boden

A scholarship? Her mom had never even mentioned that part before. For Natalie's entire life, her mom had made vague references to how she'd gone off to the city to start her acting career, but she'd never discussed the fact that she'd actually studied theater. She'd gotten off to a much better start in her career than

Natalie had. Who knows how far she could have gone? What kind of parts she could have gotten?

But none of it had happened. She'd lost out on her dreams when she'd gotten pregnant and married her dad. Natalie had experienced a small taste of that kind of disappointment, but her mom had lived through years and years of it.

She continued sorting boxes, but her mind wasn't focused on the task anymore. In her memory, she was wandering through her childhood and beyond, through moments and behavior patterns she'd always resented: her mom's harshness and criticism, her frequent irritability. These were things she'd approached with some bitter sense that her mom just didn't get her or have much regard for her. But now she saw them for what they were: manifestations of her mother's deep unhappiness and, most likely, her desire to see Natalie do more with her life.

She leaned her head back against the sofa and groaned. She really had been the most self-absorbed person in the world.

After a few moments of lamenting that fact, she murmured a prayer for forgiveness, then stood and pushed the boxes away. That was enough of memory lane for one day.

Standing up, she checked her watch. It was a little over an hour until her mom got off work. Just enough time.

29

Natalie added diced chicken from the leftover Chinese food to a skillet. She'd already added vegetables from the freezer to augment the takeout broccoli and mushrooms and heated them all in oil. Next, she had added egg and the residual fried rice. The chicken was the final touch to her impromptu stir-fry.

The mixture was well heated and ready to serve by the time the front door rattled to announce her mom's return.

"Mom, I'm in here," she called over her shoulder when the door opened.

There was a rustle in the doorway then, "Natalie, what's going on?"

Natalie turned. "I decided to make dinner. The table's all set if you want some."

Her mom's eyes widened. "Oh! Well, thanks. I'm not about to turn down a hot meal. Give me a second to go get washed up."

A few minutes later, they were seated at the dining table.

"You spruced up the leftovers, huh?"

"Yeah. I added some stuff and turned it into a stir-fry."

Her mom pushed the food around her plate. "Good thinking. If you put that much effort into your career, you might be a star."

Natalie's hand gripped her fork convulsively, but she managed to force down an angry retort. She drew in a deep breath and released it as a hollow laugh. "Yeah, I guess I'll try that sometime."

A slight grimace that looked surprisingly like regret flashed across her mom's face, but she looked down quickly and took a bite. "Mm. That's good."

"Thanks."

After a few minutes of eating in silence, Natalie glanced up to find her mom watching her. Natalie sent her a small smile.

Her mom chuckled awkwardly and gestured at the table. "You know, I can't remember the last time I ate in here. I usually just have dinner in front of the TV."

"Yeah, the places I've lived have either had tiny tables or no dining space at all. This is nice."

The silence returned. This time, she was the one studying her mom. She really did seem more tired than usual.

Natalie bit her lip. She hated to shatter the calm by nagging, but concern pressed her forward. "Mom, have you given any thought to retirement plans?"

Her mom slowly finished chewing. "I think about it now and then. But I don't know what I would do. I've been at this job for over thirty years now."

"I know, but you could do other things. Find a hobby, maybe?"

Her mom rolled her eyes. "That's great, Natalie. A hobby! Maybe I could go to the senior center for bingo night."

Natalie started to bristle, as she always did at her mom's sarcasm, but suddenly an image sprang to mind of her mom at senior bingo night, trying to fend off advances from octogenarian men. A slight giggle escaped her. "No, that's not what I meant. But there must be something else."

"There is something …"

Natalie scooted closer to the table. "Yes?"

"You know the old Brighton Theater?"

Did she! How many times had she snuck into the old condemned theater and pretended to perform on the dusty stage when she was in middle school and junior high?

"Yeah. What about it?"

"It's silly, really, but Betty wants me to partner with her in restoring it and opening it again."

"Mom! That's a great idea!"

"It's just a thought," she said, with a wave of her hand. "It sounds risky. Not to mention a lot of work."

"I'm sure. But it's a lot of work on something you actually want to do, for a change."

Her mom gave a half smile. "I'll think about it."

The next morning, Natalie sipped her coffee, surveyed the remaining boxes in the living room, and endeavored to wrap her mind around the previous night's dinner with her mom. After the discussion about the old theater, they had addressed other topics—all of them uncharacteristically peaceful. What exactly had shifted between them?

Ordinarily, when sitting down to a meal with her mom, she would expect at least a few fireworks.

Suddenly, she paused and sank onto the sofa. *She would expect ...* Expectation. Maybe that was the key. For the first time since she could remember, she had approached an encounter with her mom with very few expectations.

Having felt convicted after the previous day's discoveries, she had decided to try to do something nice for her mom by having dinner ready when she came home. And for once, she hadn't spent the entire time weighing her mom's behavior against what she thought it should be or what she wanted it to be. It felt like a small but crucial first step to learning how to accept her mom as she truly was.

She took a long sip of her coffee and set it down on a coaster on the end table. Wow! Those were some pretty heavy revelations for so early in the morning.

Returning her attention to the task at hand, she slid off the sofa and resumed her place on the floor next to the pile of boxes. As she did, she noticed a notebook partially sticking out from underneath the end table. She must've left it out the day before by mistake.

The cover read, "Diane Lawson: English Composition."

It might be fun to see what high school kids wrote about in her mom's day. She thumbed through the pages. Most of the writing pertained to required reading assignments. Nothing new there.

But then she turned to a page with a black and white picture of Natalie Wood attached to it. The accompanying essay was titled, "My Future Life."

Her heart ached as she read the first paragraph, in which high school Diane described her aspirations of becoming a successful Hollywood actress.

Then the second paragraph began, "I suppose at some point I will have to have a husband."

Natalie chuckled at the lack of enthusiasm.

"But I do know," the essay continued, "that I will have a pretty little baby girl. I want to name her Natalie after my favorite actress."

Natalie's head snapped back. *She* had been part of her mom's dreams too?

A pretty little baby girl. I want to name her Natalie…

It felt inauthentic, like a glaring anachronism in a historical play.

Shakily, she closed the notebook, returned it to its box, and shoved the lot away.

After taking a final gulp to drain her coffee cup, she moved on to the next box. As soon as she opened it, the now familiar smell of musty fabric accosted her senses.

This time, the culprit was a small stack of baby clothes. There were bonnets, pink and yellow rompers and even a few toddler-sized dresses.

Beneath the clothing was a shoebox, so she preemptively covered her nose in anticipation of finding an old, mildewy pair of sneakers. To her relief, though, the box was filled with dozens of pictures.

Although there was little organization, most of them were of her when she was small. She sifted through the photos until one caught her attention. It was an old Polaroid of her mom holding her when she was around one year old.

It captured her mom's side profile as she stood holding Natalie against her shoulder with their faces nestled together. Her mom's eyes were closed in an expression that could only be described as pure joy, as if holding her child was the most wonderful thing in the world.

After a long time of staring at the image, her eyes finally traveled down to the bottom of the photo, where her mom had written "Dancing cheek to cheek with my girl."

The words pulled back the curtain on a long-hidden memory. She was small, wrapped snug and safe in her mom's arms while her melodic voice hummed, "Cheek to Cheek."

That's right! Her mom used to sing to her and dance her around the room all the time. How could she have forgotten that?

****

"It's a Polaroid," Betty observed dryly when Natalie showed up at the diner during the lull between the breakfast and lunch rushes and handed her the picture.

"Yes, I know."

Betty put on her glasses to study it closer. "Aw, that's a great shot." She returned the picture to Natalie. "What about it?"

Natalie struggled to verbalize her confusion. "It's just that Mom looked so … happy."

Betty lowered her eyes and her face saddened as she ambled toward one of the counter stools. Sitting down, she patted a seat beside her, and Natalie accepted it. "Your mom was so proud of you when she brought you into the world. Some of the old gargoyles in town were rude and judgmental because she and your dad didn't get married until just before you were born. But she didn't mind. It didn't stop her from taking you with her everywhere and showing you around. Oh, Natalie, she doted on you: talked to you, read to you, everything a perfect little mother would do."

"I barely remember," Natalie admitted. "So what happened?"

"I think she started to change when your dad left."

Natalie chewed on that for a minute. "She was hurt because she loved him so much?"

It was one of the few times she had ever seen Betty look truly uncomfortable. "I … suppose that was some of it, yes. But there were other things. Not only was there taking care of you, but your grandfather died around the same time too, you know. Before that, his hardware store had been struggling for years. He left Diane his house, but he'd had to refinance it to help his store a few years before that. Diane worked like a dog to keep the house. She was too stubborn to accept help, too.

"I guess you could say she went into survival mode. All she was able to think about was working and keeping everything running. It sharpened her edges. A lot of other things seemed to fall by the wayside."

Betty's eyes grew wistful. "She used to be soft, perceptive, and funny … she was so funny sometimes. We used to be friends, you know?"

Natalie blinked. "Really? She barely ever came over here when I was growing up, even when I worked here."

"Yeah, our friendship fell by the wayside too."

Natalie squeezed Betty's warm, firm hand. "She told me your idea about the theater. I think that would be amazing. Maybe if she had a project doing something she's passionate about, she wouldn't feel like everything is a struggle anymore. Maybe she could relax, even."

Betty nodded. "Maybe. Just remember, sweetie, it won't be a fix-all."

"What do you mean?"

"I mean, Diane won't up and retire, take on something new, and suddenly become the mom you want her to be."

Natalie looked down at the counter, tracing a crack in the tiled surface with her fingertip. "I understand that, and it's okay. I just want to see her do something that makes her happy." Her voice cracked. "I can't even remember seeing her happy."

Betty put an arm around her shoulders. "I *can* remember. That's why I want her to do it too."

30

Natalie left Betty's on her bicycle, pedaling hard enough to make the wheels turn as fast as the wheels in her head.

Betty's explanation of what her mom had gone through had helped clarify a lot. She'd known things had been difficult, but she hadn't realized the extent. One thing was certain, though: deep down, it was love and concern for her that had driven her mom.

She slowed her pace as she let that realization sink in. Her mom had always worked to take care of her, although Natalie had failed to fully recognize it for years.

Veering off the well-worn path in the woods near the diner, she brought her bike to a full stop. Maybe that same desire to take care of her was one of the things keeping her mom from jumping off and pursuing a dream of her own. Maybe she was waiting for Natalie to get her life together.

She leaned on her handlebars and closed her eyes, striving to pray … and to listen. A soft breeze stirred around her, rustling the tree branches and allowing lively beams of sunshine to trickle through. The light seemed to wrap around her, and she embraced it for many long moments.

At last, her eyes flew open. Her skin was prickling.

As fast as she could, she pedaled until she reached a clearing where she'd have a cell signal. Then she pulled out her phone and dialed.

It rang twice before Marlowe answered with a sharp "What?"

She took a deep breath and dove in. "Hey, Marlowe, it's Natalie

Rivers."

There was a long pause, followed by: "You can't be serious! Give me one good reason not to hang up on you right now."

"Okay, how about the fact that you haven't done it already?"

He snorted in response.

Still not hanging up. That was good. "How are the play preparations going?"

"If you must know, your understudy just broke her leg. And Linda, the only swing actor who was even remotely prepared enough has come down with shingles, of all things! Basically, the first preview is happening in three days without a lead, and it's all your fault!"

"I can do the play, Marlowe."

He paused again and muttered angry yet indistinguishable words under his breath. "Okay, fine. I'm desperate enough to have a stuffed ragdoll learn the lines for this preview. But I'll settle for you."

Natalie bit back a laugh. She had to admit, that was a pretty good burn.

"But you'd better be here tomorrow morning!"

"I will."

"Good."

"And Marlowe?"

"What?"

"I'm sorry."

"Whatever. Just don't make *me* sorry I answered the phone." With that, he ended the call.

****

Natalie spent the next couple of hours finishing her task of organizing the boxes in her mom's living room and tidying up the house.

By the time her mom walked in, the house was in order, and Natalie had her suitcases packed and gathered near the door.

Her mom entered the living room, looked at the luggage and then at Natalie. "What's going on?"

"I got a lead in a play, and I need to be there for rehearsal tomorrow morning."

"Oh." Her mom wrapped her arms around her middle. "That was a short visit."

Natalie took a step closer. "I'm sorry about that. But listen, I want you to visit me. My part in this play isn't exactly secure at the moment. The director hates me, and the whole thing could be a disaster, but if we pull it off and the show keeps running, I'm sending tickets for you and Betty to come to a performance. And who knows? Maybe you'll get some inspiration for opening the theater."

Her mom raised an eyebrow. "You're not gonna let that go, are you?"

Natalie chuckled. "No way!"

A small smile crossed her face. "Okay." Then she studied the bags again. "Which train are you taking back to the city?"

"The 3:40."

"I'll drive you to the station."

During the short trip to the station, Natalie answered her mom's questions about the play and her role. When they arrived, her mom helped her carry her bags up the stairs to the outdoor train platform. They made it just as the train started to pull in.

Natalie faced her mom. "Thanks for the ride. I'll call you soon, okay?"

"Okay."

She turned to move closer to the train as it slowed to a stop.

"Natalie!" her mom called out urgently.

When Natalie turned again, her mom's forehead crinkled. She opened her mouth, hedged then pressed her lips together. Hurrying forward, she wrapped her arms around Natalie in a hug.

Natalie froze for a half second then returned the embrace, squeezing her eyes shut. When she pulled back, she said, "Things are going to get better, Mom. I promise."

31

When Natalie returned to the city, she began three days of the most frantic string of dress rehearsals and last minute production preparations she'd ever experienced in her nearly fifteen years of acting.

It was exhilarating.

Fortunately, even before she'd walked off the play, she already knew her lines well enough to do them off book, but she still needed to rehearse with the rest of the cast and learn how the scenes were blocked.

She ran through her scene with Ryan a few times without freezing up, and she was almost certain it played much better too. Marlowe had given little feedback, which meant he either agreed with her or knew he didn't have time to be too exacting.

While she may have made it through rehearsals without getting panicky, she wasn't so fortunate the night of the first performance. As she sat in her dressing room a good fifty minutes before the show, her breathing was shaky and her heart was beating so hard that if it didn't slow down by the time she took the stage, the entire front row would probably hear it.

"Okay, calm down, Natalie. It's only the first preview," she murmured, trying to take comfort in the fact that this performance would have no critics yet, and they would still have time to make adjustments before opening night in a couple of weeks.

Of course, she couldn't really think of it as *only* a first preview. The previews were often the time when people with families came to the theater for a chance to see a play when tickets were the most affordable. They were also a good time for real enthusiasts to show up. She had met theatergoers who would buy tickets to several previews *and* opening night just so they could watch how the play changed and evolved in the process. To her, pleasing these groups of patrons was every bit as crucial as impressing the critics.

Finally, she closed her eyes and bowed her head. Her thoughts turned to the prayer she had seen in Darla's prayer book only that morning. It was a prayer of self-dedication, for giving everything like thoughts and imagination over to God and asking him to use them for his glory.

After a moment's reflection, she whispered, "God, I'm not 100 percent sure what I'm doing here tonight. Betty was right; your love is transforming me. I know it. But you didn't take away my desire to be here and to keep practicing this craft, so I have to think that maybe you want me to use it somehow. Please guide me to use all of this as you want me to, and help me to live in your love. Amen."

Her eyes remained closed, and a strange peace settled around her.

"Hey, Natalie." She raised her head and turned toward the open dressing room door, where Ryan was standing. His cheeks reddened. "Oh, I'm sorry to interrupt while you're preparing."

"That's okay. I don't really get into character until the half." Truthfully, this probably would've been a good time to give herself more than thirty minutes, but there was no need to be rude. Her lack of foresight wasn't Ryan's fault.

"I wanted to say I'm really glad to be working with you again. And I don't know what was going on before, but it's really impressive how you made it back and got ready so fast. You're one of the best actors I've worked with so far and ..." His color deepened and he lowered his eyes. "I'm sorry to ramble."

She stood up and gave him a reassuring pat on the shoulder. He really was a sweet kid. "That's very kind of you, Ryan. Thank you."

He turned to leave, but then did an about-face. "By the way, I didn't know you were religious."

"It's a fairly recent development," she admitted.

"Is that why you came back?"

"You could say that ..."

"I'm sorry. I don't mean to pry. I was just interested."

"I don't mind." She paused, seized by impulsive curiosity. "Do you believe in God, Ryan?"

"I do, actually." He chuckled. "Not only that, I think he plays jokes on me."

"What do you mean?"

"For one thing, my dad is Donny French."

Her mouth fell open. "As in, multi-Tony award-winning Donny French?"

"Yeah. I changed my last name because he and I don't really get along. When I grew up, I didn't want anything to do with the crazy lifestyle his career built."

"But … you're an actor."

"Right? And there's one joke. I found out I really enjoy performing."

"You have talent, for sure."

His face reddened again. "Thanks. I knew I had to give it a try. So I auditioned and took whatever parts I could get, but this is the biggest one so far."

"In a play about the dysfunctional families of actors."

He guffawed. "Exactly! And it's so true to life. I knew plenty of Liams growing up. This whole thing has forced me to relive memories. It was almost enough to make me quit. But I stuck it out because I realized it was helping me process."

"So it was a *good* joke?"

"Yeah, I guess so." His face grew thoughtful. "And you know what really convinced me to stay? I think it was our Liam and Marissa scene. There's hope there, you know? I keep thinking, if I found some of that hope from this side of it…"

She gestured toward the front of house. "Then maybe someone out there will too?"

His face lit up. "Maybe so."

"Thank you for sharing that with me. It's kinda given me some perspective too."

"Ladies and gentlemen of *The Seat Fillers* company, this is your half-hour call."

"Well, I guess it's time to get ready, huh, *Liam?*"

"After you, Marissa."

Natalie waited and held her breath. Was that her pulse pounding in her ears or applause? She swallowed and willed her heartbeat to settle.

Yes, the audience was definitely applauding as the rest of the cast moved center stage by singles or pairs and took their bows. Ryan went last then turned and swept his arms behind him.

Natalie glided upstage, and the claps grew louder, with several cheers and whistles added in. Tears sprang to her eyes, and she took one deep bow, then a second.

Grateful warmth throbbed through her heart as she blew a kiss to the audience.

Then she held out her hand so her castmates could join her and they could all take their bows together.

32

Natalie left the chaotic theater behind and strolled down the street without bothering to consider her direction. There were so many other things to consider, like all the little adjustments that needed to be made before the next performance. But none of that superseded the relief of getting through the first one.

When she reached a nearby bus stop that was empty, she sat down on the bench and closed her eyes. Laughter and conversation from passing pedestrians layered over one another. They all seemed to be going somewhere together. Strange, how easy it was to feel isolated in a city of eight million people.

She gave her head a shake. How ungrateful. Yes, being surrounded by couples, families, and clusters of friends was a stark reminder that she'd once again managed to find herself wandering the city with no friends or family, but she wasn't alone now. God had been with her through her nerves and fears tonight and had helped her deliver a strong performance. It wasn't right to ask any more at the moment, even if—

"Natalie! Natalie!" a small, exuberant voice yelled, snapping her out of her reverie.

She looked around for the source of the voice and did a double take. "Licha?"

The girl rushed up and threw her arms around Natalie's neck. It took a second for Natalie to recover from her shock, but once she did, she returned the embrace. "What on earth are you doing here?”

“We saw the play!” she squealed.

“We?” Standing up and moving away from the bus stop enclosure revealed half a dozen more kids. They crowded around, all chattering at once.

“I liked the play.”

“It was sooo good.”

“You’re a great actress!”

Natalie couldn’t keep the grin from her face. “You guys! This is so great. Thank you.”

“Previews are a good time for a theater field trip, don’t you think?”

She looked over the crowd of kids to where Darla stood behind them. “Darla! Hey! I can’t believe you brought the kids to see the show. How did you know I’d be in it? I didn’t even know until a few days ago.”

Darla shrugged. “Friends in the business.” She leaned closer. “By the way, your performance tonight was inspired.”

“Oh, thank you so much, Darla.” Natalie reached out and squeezed her hand. “You don’t know how glad I am to see you all.”

Her eyes swept over the kids. “In fact, what would you all say to a quick cup of ice cream? My treat.”

The kids expressed their immediate approval, but Darla pulled an exaggerated scowl. “You’re trying to stick me with six juveniles hyped up on sugar?”

“Make that seven! I’m getting extra sprinkles on mine,” Natalie fired back.

The kids dissolved into giggles. Their laughter sounded good. It was almost like being at the camp again … with one painful exception.

She didn’t have to ask where Glenn was. If the fact that she had blown him off hadn’t been enough to keep him away, then the letter would’ve most certainly done the trick.

Even though she knew it had been the right thing to do, her stomach still knotted when she thought of him reading her story.

She took an unsteady breath. “There’s an ice cream place a couple of blocks away. Why don’t you all walk ahead, and I will catch up in a minute?”

The kids scrambled to the crosswalk with Darla trailing behind them. But at the last minute, Darla turned and looked around. Her focus wasn't on Natalie, though. Finally, she glowered at some spot behind Natalie and snapped, "For heaven's sake, Glenn, don't hover in the shadows. Put on your big boy pants, and come talk to Natalie!"

Then she hurried to catch up with the kids, all the while muttering under her breath.

Natalie whirled around and searched the sidewalk behind her. Sure enough, Glenn was leaning against a wall. A tiny gasp escaped her lips as she watched him straighten and slowly approach.

He was wearing his nice suit again, with his hair carefully slicked back. His big brown eyes were searching her, as if he'd never seen her before.

Well, that couldn't be good.

She plundered her brain for something to say, but he saved her the trouble. "Natalie, you were absolutely amazing up there tonight."

That was so him: endlessly kind, no matter what.

A feeble "Thank you" was all she could manage.

He nodded once and fidgeted with the buttons on his jacket. "I'd ask for your autograph, but I guess I already have it on this." Reaching into his coat pocket, he pulled out an envelope. Her letter.

Now it was her turn to fidget. She tucked a stray strand of hair behind her ear with a shaky hand. "I—I figured after you read that, you'd stay as far away as you could."

His brow knit in confusion. "Why? Because you told me about your background? Are you kidding me? Everyone has stuff they're ashamed of." His face brightened. "Besides, that's not who you are now."

"No, but up until a few weeks ago, that's exactly who I was. I mean," she waved her hand in frustration, "half of the time we were at camp, I was pretending to be a nice person just to fit in! And, yes, something radical happened while I was there, but I still have my issues. If I didn't, I wouldn't have tried to deceive you about being involved with EJ."

He stepped forward eagerly. "Ah, but you came clean about that in your letter, right?" He studied her face. "You're not involved with him now, are you?"

"No."

The corners of his mouth lifted. "Then how about going out with me again?"

She clenched her fists and groaned. "Glenn, you are deliberately missing the point here! We aren't right for each other." She couldn't stop the slight tremor in her voice. "It's not fair to you. I have too much growing to do."

"We've all got growing to do, sweetheart."

The endearment made her heart leap in spite of itself.

He took another step forward until they were almost touching. "I'm not trying to belittle your past journey. But, as for the journey ahead of you … well, let's just say that I wouldn't want to miss a minute of it."

His voice was gentle and impossibly sweet as he echoed the same phrase she had used in her letter to him. But a hint of vulnerability shone in his eyes too, like he wondered if she'd meant what she'd written.

"I want you to level with me," he continued. "If you don't want me around, that's fine. I'll get lost and leave you alone, I promise." A flash of pain crossed his face. "But if you do, then I'm not going anywhere. I'll come to every performance of every play you're in. I'll send flowers and burnt homemade cookies to your dressing room."

She released a startled laugh, but he pressed on, unperturbed. "I'll stick around and wait it out until you're ready to find out what God could have in store for the two of us."

She stared at him, his words trickling through her and wrapping their way around her heart. Tears gathered at the edge of her vision until his face became blurry, so she dashed them away with her fingertips.

She couldn't argue with him anymore. She didn't want to. It had been this way since the very first. It didn't matter if he was asking her to cook for thirty ravenous kids or trying to convince her to throw away her reservations and reach for an uncertain future … He was irresistible.

She choked out a surrendering sob. Almost of their own accord, her arms reached for him, sliding up and around his shoulders as she pulled him into a tight hug.

His whispered, "Thank you, God," tickled her ear when he enfolded her in his arms and pressed her close. His whole frame seemed to radiate joy and acceptance, and she embraced it for all she was worth.

After a lengthy moment, he pulled away enough to look into her eyes. At first, it seemed like he wanted to speak, but instead, he leaned down and kissed her.

Her eyes closed and she kissed him back, savoring how his lips moved over hers with breathtaking tenderness, savoring the feeling of being cherished by the man she was coming to adore.

When they finally pulled away, she reached up and stroked his jawline. "Hmm, I was right. You *are* a terrific kisser."

He blinked in surprise. "Huh?"

Happy laughter bubbled up inside her. "Never mind. I'll explain later. Besides, we should really probably see about Darla and the kids."

"Oh man, you're right! I'm sure she'll understand the delay up to a point, but we better not push it. Believe me, you don't want to see Darla when she gets mad."

"I'm sure you're right, if her little 'put-on-your-big-boy-pants' speech was any indication," she said with a chuckle.

"Yeah, what a force of nature! It's hard to put on your big boy pants when somebody is kickin' you in them."

Natalie stifled a giggle then slid her arm through Glenn's and gave it a squeeze. "I can't say I'm sorry she did, though."

"Me neither," he murmured. "Okay, I'll call to make sure she knows we're on our way."

He pulled out his cell phone and dialed, but she didn't really follow the conversation until he said, "We'll be there in a couple of minutes, Darla. We're right by that fancy dry cleaner on 65th."

Curious, she looked up at his reference point and froze. Sebastian's overpriced dry cleaner! Had it really been only a month since she was last here? Memories of the day flooded back to her. The callback and floating on air.

Her silhouette was reflected in the cleaner's darkened window. The same woman ... yet changed so much.

"Darla, I gotta go. We'll see you in a minute." Glenn's reflection was beside hers now, his head bent in concern.

"Natalie, what's the matter? I have a feeling that's not your 'Oh, shoot, I forgot to pick up my dry cleaning' face."

When she faced him, his forehead was creased with deep worry lines, so she reached up to smooth them with her fingertips. "No."

Then, impulsively, she threw her head back and laughed. She

laughed like she hadn't laughed since she was a child—maybe even a baby, dancing in her mother's arms.

"No," she repeated breathlessly. "I think it's my grateful face. My loved and transformed, no-more-walls-of-Jericho grateful face!"

His jubilant laughter mingled with hers as she took his arm again, and they strolled down the vibrant city streets together.

The End

THANK YOU!

Dear reader

I hope you enjoyed Natalie's story, and that it encouraged you in your own personal walk with the Lord. You'll find further inspiration and encouragement on The Potter's House Books Website, (www.pottershousebooks.com) and by reading the other books in the series. Read them all and be encouraged and uplifted!

Find all the books on Amazon and on The Potter's House Books website.

If you enjoyed *Changed Somehow*, please consider leaving a review on Amazon or Goodreads.

I'd also love to connect on Facebook, Twitter, or BookBub. Also, don't forget to check out my author newsletter, where I talk about my books and the books and authors I admire.

Blessings!
Chloe

ACKNOWLEDGMENTS

I am so grateful to my fellow Potter's House Series 2 authors. It is humbling to be on a team with these talented, spirit-led writers. A big thanks also goes to Becky, not only for her VA superpowers, but also for her constant encouragement; to Marion for the beautiful cover design; and to my proofreader Tracy for her precise and thorough work.

I'm also thankful for my family, brothers and sisters in Christ, and friends who have given me so much love and support as I was writing this. I want to give a special shout-out to my beta readers, Valerie, Wendy, and Paula. In addition, I want to thank Alicia and Donna for helping me come up with the name, "Sebastian Claypool," and Lauren for her theater expertise. In addition, thank you to the lovely friends on my street team. You all have been such a blessing.

I'm also grateful for the musical inspiration of The Hot Sardines, whose scintillating rhythms helped keep the creative juices flowing as I wrote this book.

Most of all, I want to thank my Creator for the countless ways He reveals His grace day after day.

ABOUT THE AUTHOR

Chloe S. Flanagan is an author, technical writer, blogger, and graduate of New York University. She enjoys exploring the Christian walk frankly and thoughtfully in her fiction and in her blog, The Candid Corinthian. When she's not writing, Chloe loves music, travel, reading books in all genres, and spending time with family.

Other books by Chloe S. Flanagan:

An Offer of Grace: A Christian Romantic Suspense Series

Forward to What Lies Ahead

A Time for Every Matter

No Longer a Stranger